GAME OVER,

PETE WATSON

GAME OVER, PETE WATSON

JOE SCHREIBER
illustrated by ANDY RASH

Houghton Mifflin Harcourt
Boston   New York

www.hmhco.com
The text of this book is set in Linotype New Century Schoolbook.

Library of Congress Cataloging-in-Publication Data
Schreiber, Joe, 1969–
Game over, Pete Watson / by Joe Schreiber.
p. cm.
Summary: "When videogame obsessed Pete Watson discovers his dad is not only a super-spy but has been kidnapped and is now trapped inside a video game, he has to use his super gaming skills and enter the game to rescue him. And if he succeeds, who will save Pete from his massive crush on Callie Midwood?"
—Provided by publisher.
ISBN 978-0-544-15756-9 (hardback)
[1. Video games—Fiction. 2. Spies—Fiction. 3. Humorous stories.] I. Title.
PZ7.S37913Gam 2014
[Fic]—dc23
2013024335

Manufactured in U.S.A.
DOC 10 9 8 7 6 5 4 3 2 1

4500459362

To my kids, who sat at the dining room table reading this book off my laptop and laughing out loud.

GAME OVER, PETE WATSON

[CHAPTER ONE]
I'M SORRY, OKAY?

On the Saturday morning that I almost triggered the end of the world, I woke up early. I was excited for three reasons:

1) No school.
2) Mom and Dad would be at Dad's company softball game, which meant that I would have the house to myself all day.
3) **BRAWL-A-THON 3000 XL!!!!**

The original Brawl-A-Thon 3000 is my favorite video game of all time. If you asked me to rank my top ten games, it would go something like this:

1) Brawl-A-Thon 3000
2) Santa's Go-Kart Apocalypse
3) Galactic Sheep-Sheep
4) Galactic Sheep-Sheep Returns
5) Maynard GermQuake's Return to ToxiCity
6) Ninja Geeks: Fist of Algebra

7) Doctor Dragon's Dojo of Doom
8) Unicorn Zombies
9) Tomb of the Penguin Warlord
10) Mr. Thumb Goes to Market (it's better than it sounds)

The exact order might change based on how I'm feeling that day, but trust me, Brawl-A-Thon 3000 is always at the top of the list.

Now I know there's more to life than video games. You have to have laptops and iPhones too, so you can download apps and watch videos and take pictures and write books like this one, which I couldn't even type up without my mom's laptop. I'm also going to use the drawing program, because a picture is worth a thousand words, and I want this book to be at least fifty thousand words long, so I figure fifty pictures ought to do it.

ONLY 49,000 TO GO!

The point is, I'm not one of those guys who's just going to sit here and tell you that video games are the only things that matter.

[CHAPTER TWO]

VIDEO GAMES:
THE ONLY THINGS
THAT MATTER

The original Brawl-A-Thon 3000 is the single greatest video game in history. In fact, the experts all agree that it's pretty much the reason that video games were invented in the first place. Yes, *it's that good*.

First of all, imagine parachuting down onto this half-destroyed island where packs of vicious half-mechanical animals have taken over. You have to build a character out of all these leftover machines and animal parts and fight an army of mutant machine beasts called MechReatures.

Also, on this island time flows backwards *and* forward so that one minute you might be tearing a MechReature apart and the next minute you're accidentally building it up again. There are all kinds of mini games along the way where you have to shoot poison weeds and play speed chess against superintelligent monkey MechReatures. At the end of every level you have to battle a Mega-MechReature who is made up of all the worst parts of the guys you just fought. And that's just the beginning.

Dad says there's more to life than video games and nobody ever made the world a better place by battling mechanical wolves and laser-eyed hyenas all day, and I guess everybody's entitled to their opinion.

But I have been playing Brawl-A-Thon 3000 for three years and I have gotten farther than anybody else I know, except for Wesley Midwood, who used to be my best friend.

What happened?

It's a long and tragic story.

[CHAPTER THREE]
WESLEY MIDWOOD AND THE SPITTY MOUTH BANJO OF DOOM

Wesley's a little weird. He's a little overweight and has huge teeth. He's the kind of kid who not only has rubber bands in his braces but has learned how to play them with his tongue, like a banjo. Sometimes in the cafeteria he'll say, really loud, "How about a little 'Dueling Tonsils'?" and open his mouth and start wiggling his tongue, just strumming those rubber bands. It sounds a little like this:

Twang
Twang
Twang!
Blunka
Blunka-
Blunka!

In the deluxe digital edition of this book you'll be able to click on the picture and hear the sound it made. For now, just imagine banjos but with a lot more spit. You get the idea.

That's not what ruined the friendship, though. If you want the embarrassing truth about that, you're going to have to keep reading.

Those days, Mom was always asking me why I didn't invite Wesley over, and I had to keep making up excuses like Wesley was busy or he had the mumps or something. The fact is, I was running out of reasons, and I kept hoping Wesley and his family might just move away, but that didn't seem like it was going to happen any time soon either. See, Wesley's dad was my dad's boss at Health Solutions Inc., the company where he worked, and I guess Mr. Midwood had just gotten a big promotion. Dad kept talking about it at dinner while he was cutting his steak into too many little pieces and squeaking his fork on the plate from pushing on it too hard or something.

I tried not to ask questions.

Like I said, I stick to video games.

[CHAPTER FOUR]

THE STICKY NOTE THAT DESTROYED EVERYTHING

By the way, if I didn't already mention it, **BRAWL-A-THON 3000 XL** was coming out today.

I could spend all day telling you why it's so cool, but basically the quick version is that it features whole new mutant strains and weapons and levels that take place on different planets and it looks totally amazing. Also, in this version time doesn't just move backwards and forward; it also moves sideways, which means if you're not careful, you might just erase yourself from existence.

Plus, like the title implies, all the creatures are *extra large*.

It cost $49.99, and I had been saving up for it for the past two months. My plan this morning was to wait for Mom and Dad to leave, then ride my bike down to Ready Player One, which is the video game store by the mall, and buy the game, then on the way back "lose" the receipt so I couldn't return it. It wasn't that Mom and Dad disapproved of it, exactly, but they were always asking me if I thought video games were a "wise use of my money." They also talk a lot about buyer's remorse, which I've had only once, when I spent my money on a pair of binoculars for Boy Scouts, and I definitely wasn't going to repeat *that* mistake.

I waited until the house was quiet and went downstairs. Mom had left three pieces of french toast for me, and I ate them while I checked my Brawl-A-Thon jar, counting out the cash into piles. So far, so good. But before I could finish counting, I found a little yellow sticky note tucked in the bottom. It said:

Pete:
I.O.U. $20.⁰⁰
Love You!
Mom

For a second I just sat there with the note in my hand. I couldn't believe this was actually happening.

I mean, okay, Mom occasionally "borrows" money from my jar when she needs cash to tip the paper boy or pay for the Girl Scout cookies that she forgot she ordered. She always pays me back as soon as she gets to the bank. But today was the worst possible time for that to happen.

I needed an idea, fast.

First I checked under all the couch cushions, because sometimes you can find spare change inside there, but all I got was an old pen, some baseball cards that I thought I'd lost, three nickels, and a thick black Magic Marker. I thought about going out to see if anybody had lost a dog or a cat and trying to bring it back for a reward, but that was going to take too much time, and I didn't think anybody in our neighborhood had lost a pet lately anyway.

I picked up the Magic Marker, turned around, and practically tripped over the leftover pizza box from last night sitting next to the trash can.

That's when it hit me.

The Magic Marker. The pizza box.

It was a sign.

[CHAPTER FIVE]
THE SIGN

It was just four words written on the torn-off flap of the pizza box, but right away I knew it was the answer.

HUG GARAGE SALE TODAY!

I carried it outside and taped it to our mailbox. Then I went back into the house and started looking for things to sell. That would give people time to notice the sign and build anticipation. Like they say in the business world, "Sell the sizzle, not the steak."

Our basement didn't have much in the way of

sizzle or steak, but it was full of stuff that nobody ever used anymore, like an old treadmill, a guinea pig cage, and the home soda-making machine we'd gotten Dad for Christmas two years ago. He'd only used it once and made us all try "Dad's Old-Time Homemade Root Beer." After I had three glasses and got sick, Dad put it away in the corner and covered it up with a blanket. If all the parts were still there, I figured that alone was worth at least twenty bucks, easy.

In the end, the basement turned out to be a gold mine. I grabbed an old pair of skis, along with some clothes and coats and stuff, a Hot Wheels set with almost all the pieces, and six boxes of dusty books. I rounded out the selection with some collectible Rocket Lad cups and souvenir mugs from our last trip to Florida. It took me about twenty minutes to get it all up to the garage and set it out on two card tables and a blanket spread out in the driveway.

I really didn't think Mom and Dad would mind if I got rid of some of this stuff. Mom had wanted to participate in the big neighborhood yard sale last spring, but Dad had said the last thing he felt like doing on his day off was watch a bunch of strangers paw through our stuff and make comments about it.

The way I saw it, I was doing everybody a favor.
I waited for the money to start rolling in.

[CHAPTER SIX]

THE MONEY DOES NOT ROLL IN

An hour later, the only person that had even stopped to look was our neighbor Mrs. Wertley, who was walking her dog, Mr. Yappers. Mrs. Wertley is a retired English teacher, and she stood there looking at the souvenir coffee mugs that I put out and telling me about her trip to the Everglades last year to see her grandchildren. I think she was scaring my other customers away. She didn't even buy anything.

"If you really want to earn some money," she said, "you could come and mow my lawn. I'll pay you five dollars and all the iced tea you can drink."

I said no thanks. I'd made that mistake once before, when I'd really needed cash for Galactic Sheep-Sheep Returns and offered to clean out her garage for five dollars. It was the hardest five dollars I'd ever made. The entire time that I was cleaning, Mrs. Wertley kept asking me questions and correcting my grammar. She brought out a copy of *Warriner's English Grammar and Composition,* and she said it was the most valuable thing that she owned.

"If I had to be stranded on a desert island with just one book, it would be this one," she said. "I never leave home without it, and neither should you."

I thought that if I had to be stranded on a desert island with just one book, it would be a giant inflatable waterproof bath book that I could use as a raft to float away on, but I didn't say anything.

"Uh-huh," I said.

"That's the trouble with youth these days," she said. "They all think they deserve a free ride. Don't you pay any attention to what's happening in the world today?"

"Not really," I said.

"Of course not," she said. "You're the iPod generation, and you just want to keep your heads in the iClouds."

"Uh-huh," I said.

"'Uh-huh,'" she said. "That's one word that you won't find in *Warriner's English Grammar and Composition.*"

"Right," I said.

On the way down the driveway, she turned around and said, "Oh, and you spelled 'huge' wrong, Pete."

UNLESS YOU WANT ME TO GIVE YOU A BIG "HUG"!

Meanwhile it was almost eleven o'clock already and I hadn't made a single sale.

I was getting desperate. I went back inside to see if there was anything else worth selling. When I got down to the basement, I moved some stuff around and pulled another box from out of the corner. It was old and dusty, and it took me a second to even realize what was in it.

Written in faded red letters across the box was **COMMANDROID 85 VIDEO ARCADE SYSTEM.**

It was the old game console that Dad had had when he was a kid. He never took it out, and I knew he'd never even miss it. He probably didn't even remember it was here. I'd be doing him a favor getting rid of it.

I also found an old TV that we never used anymore. I carried it upstairs along with the CommandRoid and set the TV up in the driveway. There was a long extension cord in the garage, and I plugged the TV in. I figured this way at least I wouldn't get bored while I waited. Without cable, though, it didn't work out so well.

I was about to hook up the CommandRoid when everything changed.

[CHAPTER SEVEN]

THE RETURN OF
WESLEY MIDWOOD

It all started when a van pulled up in front of my driveway. At first I was excited that I actually had a customer, until I realized who it was.

Wesley Midwood jumped out of the back and ran over to me while his mom sat behind the wheel.

"Hey, Pete!" He looked around at all the stuff, and then stared right at the sign that said GARAGE SALE.

WHAT IS THIS, SOME KIND OF GARAGE SALE OR SOMETHING?

"Yeah," I said. "That's the idea."

"Whoa, these are cool!" He picked up a pair of x-ray specs and put them on. "Do they really work?"

"Sure they do. Take them home and see. Two bucks."

"Really? I'll go ask my mom." He started to run back to the van, and I got nervous, because all of a sudden I remembered that the x-ray specs actually belonged to him and he'd left them at my house a couple of years ago. If his mom figured that out, it would be no sale, and I might have to give them back for free.

Then I saw something that made me forget all about the x-ray specs.

Wesley's older sister, Callie, was sitting in the passenger seat of the van, staring straight at me.

Which means I can't put it off any longer. This is the embarrassing part.

Read the next chapter if you dare.

Just don't say I didn't warn you.

[CHAPTER EIGHT]
THE EMBARRASSING CHAPTER

Okay, I'm going to tell this part fast to get it over with. You have to know it in order to understand the rest of the story, but I don't want to drag it out any more than I absolutely have to. You'll understand once you read it.

Callie is seventeen. She used to be my babysitter back when I was in fourth grade, which is the last year I needed a babysitter. She has red hair and green eyes and drives a purple car and has this way of laughing that I can't describe except it makes my heart beat faster every time she does it and my palms get sweaty and I kind of forget how to breathe.

I don't exactly know when I started having a crush on her, but when she used to come babysit, she'd read me the dumbest, most babyish books ever, and I'd sit there not even caring. Other times she'd sit at our kitchen table and do her math homework, and I'd try to help her with the story problems.

I should have known it couldn't last. The good times never do.

This is how it all fell apart. One time when she was over babysitting, making popcorn for us, she caught me drawing a picture. I'll show it to you once, and never again. This is what it looked like:

I didn't even realize that Callie was looking over my shoulder when I drew it. The next thing I knew, I heard her saying: "Is that supposed to be *me?*"

I crumpled it up and ran upstairs to my room and didn't come out for the rest of the night. In the morning I told my mom I didn't want Callie to come and babysit anymore. Mom said that that was crazy, that Callie was the best babysitter I'd ever had. So finally I made up a story that she'd been on the phone with her boyfriend the whole time she was over and I didn't feel like she was doing a very good job keeping me safe.

That did the trick. Mom never hired Callie to come over again.

Anyway, she must have found out why we never invited her back, because even from the back of the van, her glare didn't look friendly.

Wesley came back over with the x-ray specs in his hand. "My mom says I can't buy these," he said. "She said I had a pair just like them and I must have lost them somewhere."

"Huh," I said. "That's too bad."

"Yeah," he said. "You got anything else cool here?"

I was trying to think of a polite way to ask him if he was actually going to buy anything when he saw the CommandRoid sitting on the table. "Hey, my dad's got one of those too!"

"Oh yeah?"

"Yeah. It's really old and boring."

"I know," I said. "I can't believe they ever played those things."

"They have these controllers called joysticks," Wesley said. "They're super hard to use."

"No doubt," I said, and I was starting to remember why I liked to hang out with Wesley before. Even though his sister had totally humiliated me, he was the only guy I could really talk to about video games.

"Hey," he said, "you know what comes out today?"

"Brawl-A-Thon 3000 XL," I said. "I'm going to go buy it as soon as I get some money."

His eyes got huge again. "Really?"

"Absolutely."

"That's so—"

Wesley's mom honked the horn and gestured over at him, and Wesley nodded. "Oh yeah," he said. "I almost forgot why I came over." He reached into his pocket and handed me a folded-up invitation. There was a picture of the Mario Brothers, and it said:

"What's this?" I asked.

"It's my birthday," Wesley said. "Mom said I could have a sleepover tonight in the basement! Think you can come?"

"I don't know," I said, looking around at the garage sale. "I'm kind of busy."

"Nabeel Sarwani is going to be there, and Rashaad Strong and Squid Mancini. We're going to have a cooler of two-liters and Doritos and pizza, and my mom says we can stay up all night watching scary movies and playing video games."

"Nabeel?" I looked at him. "And *Squid?*"

"Squid can hypnotize people," Wesley said. "And Nabeel can do human beatbox. He's really good." Wesley cupped his hands to his mouth and starting making beatbox noises into them. Mainly it sounded really spitty. "I can't do it as good as he does, though."

I didn't say anything. Maybe it was just because I hadn't known Wesley was hanging out with anybody at school. I definitely wasn't jealous, that's for sure.

"I can't," I said. "Sorry."

"Check with your mom," Wesley said. "Maybe she'll say yes."

"I doubt it."

Wesley twanged his rubber bands some more. "Can you at least ask?"

"Probably not." I had forgotten how annoying Wesley could be when he wanted something. "They're at that company softball game all day. You know, the one that your dad is at too?" I was hoping to maybe make him feel a little guilty about the fact that my dad might actually be here if Wesley's dad weren't making him play softball, but Wesley didn't seem to get that part, because he just stuck out his lip and started twanging his rubber bands again. *Twang-twang-twang, blunka-blunka-blunka.*

"Okay, well . . ." He looked back at the van where his mom and his sister were waiting. "I guess I'll see you later."

"Yeah," I said. "See you at school."

Wesley walked away. And I felt a little bad about it, because we were still kind of friends, I guess, but there was no way I was going back to his house when Callie was there. I thought about the drawer in my dresser upstairs, where I'd stashed the drawing I did of us two years ago.

As soon as I got the chance, I was definitely going to throw it out.

[CHAPTER NINE]

NEVER TRUST A GUY WITH A GIANT BUG ON HIS CAR

It was almost noon, and I was getting ready to pack it in when the Bug Man pulled up.

He drove a big red van with a huge cockroach on the roof and words on the side. It looked something like this:

The driver's door opened and a cheerful guy in an orange and white exterminator's jumpsuit and a green cap got out and walked up the driveway toward me, whistling under his bushy mustache. He looked like the kind of guy who stops at garage sales all the time, just to see what they have.

"Hey, there, sport," the Bug Man said. "Selling off the old family heirlooms?"

I just nodded.

"Lots of great stuff here. Yes, sir." His eyes were bright blue, and they skimmed across the tables of stuff I'd put out. "Real collector's items, I bet, right? Nice."

Then he stopped, and I realized he was looking at the CommandRoid. He walked over to it slowly, like it was an animal that might run away. He reached down and picked it up. His voice was different now, softer.

"Hey," he said. "This belong to you, sport?"

"My dad."

"Your old man know you're selling it?"

I took in a breath. "He doesn't care. He never plays it anyway." I almost told the Bug Man that I wasn't even sure it worked, but he already looked too interested and I didn't want to ruin a chance for my only sale. "It's pretty old," I said.

"You bet it is," the Bug Man said, but he wasn't even looking at me anymore. His attention was totally fixed on the CommandRoid. "In fact, I haven't seen one like this in a very long time." He raised an eyebrow. "How much do you want for it?"

I'd put a ten-dollar price tag on it, but either he must not have seen it or he was trying to bargain me down. I decided to take a chance. "Ten dollars."

"Ten bucks, huh?" the Bug Man said. "You firm on that?"

"What?"

"That means . . ." He smiled, but it was a strange, tight smile that didn't really come up to his eyes. "Are you *open to negotiation?*"

I was getting a little nervous, but something inside me wouldn't give up. "Like you said, it's a collector's item."

"Good for you, sport," the Bug Man said, and took out his wallet, slipping a twenty-dollar bill from inside. "You got change for a twenty?"

"I . . ." I hadn't even thought about making change for people. "I have to go inside and get it."

"Never mind. Keep the change." He was back to staring at the CommandRoid again, and it was like everything else around him, including me, had just disappeared. "I'm the kind of guy who sees something he wants and has to have it, never mind the price." Then he flashed me a quick smile again. "Pleasure doing business with you, sport."

"What? Oh yeah. You too." Before I could even process the twenty dollars he'd put in my hand, he was already carrying the CommandRoid back down the driveway to his van and climbing inside. Then he was gone.

[CHAPTER TEN]

HOORAY!
EVERYTHING'S
GREAT!
UNTIL IT ISN'T.

I didn't waste any time. I scribbled a note down in case Mom and Dad came home before I got back and rode my bike over to Ready Player One as fast as I could.

I'd expected a crowd, but the store didn't even look busy. The game was right there at the counter. I paid for it and crumpled up the receipt, dropping it in the trash on the way out. That was when I saw the banner over the door:

Ready Player One – A Proud Sponsor of the 14th Annual GameCon!
March 19-21, City Convention Center

I stared at it.

GameCon is huge—the biggest video game convention in the country. According to the banner, it started today. I'd read all about it online—not only were there new games that nobody had played before, but there were these giant wall-size, hundred-foot plasma screens where you could play them. Plus, as if any further awesomeness were required, the guest of honor this year was none other than Shigeru Miyamoto, the legendary creator of Zelda, Mario, Donkey Kong, and basically every good game that's ever come out for the Wii or any other game system you can think of.

Admission was something like fifty dollars a day, and it was one of those things that I knew my parents would never let me go to, so I had tried to blot it out of my memory. But now that it was here, I realized that my strategy hadn't worked. Now I understood why there wasn't anybody shopping at Ready Player One. Anybody with a car and half a brain was already at the City Convention Center, playing games that normal people probably wouldn't see for years, if ever.

Now I wished I hadn't even seen the GameCon banner. My dad says sometimes ignorance is bliss, which I always thought was stupid, until now.

When I stepped out of the store, a black car pulled up in front of me and a guy jumped out.

It was my father.

He didn't look happy. I don't remember his exact words, but they were something like:

WHAT DID YOU DO WITH THE COMMANDROID?

It looked bad, but I wasn't worried. The way I saw it, there were a couple ways I could handle this:

A) THE INNOCENT APPROACH

WHAT IS THIS "COMMANDROID"?

Dad just stood there staring at me. His voice got very quiet. "Pete," he said. "You have no idea what you've done."

It was obviously time to try another approach.

B) THE HONEST APPROACH

I HONESTLY HAVE NO IDEA WHAT YOU'RE TALKING ABOUT.

That was when I noticed Dad didn't seem so angry anymore. He just looked at me.

"Pete," he said, "no matter what happens, there's something you need to know."

In that moment a whole list of possibilities went through my mind:

1) "You were adopted from a family of gypsies who are coming back to take you home."
2) "It will cost too much to send you to college, so we're shipping you off to live in another country, where you can make cheap sneakers."
3) "Brushing your teeth doesn't actually do anything

for cavities. You're really just smearing your teeth with a special kind of white mud — it says so right on the tube. We just made you do it to see how long you'd keep it up before you finally read the tube."

4) "Your mother and I thought it would be funny to teach you to talk wrong so that every time you thought you were ordering a Coke, you were really saying, 'I made wet-wet in my nug-nugs!'"

5) "Santa Claus, the Easter Bunny, and the Tooth Fairy are all real, but they never liked you, so we've been covering for them all these years."

[CHAPTER ELEVEN]
HOWEVER . . .

Dad didn't actually say any of that stuff.

He didn't get a chance. Suddenly another black car swung up behind him, and two guys in suits yanked him into the back and drove away.

In the digital version of this book, you'll be able to click on the video and see it all happening, but right now this is the best I can do:

[CHAPTER TWELVE]

I MAKE WET-WET IN MY NUG-NUGS

Okay. This is the hardest part to tell you about. And not just because I'd seen my dad get kidnapped by two guys right in front of me and drew a really lame picture of it.

That's the main reason. But also, when I ran back inside Ready Player One to talk to the guy behind the counter who'd just sold me my copy of Brawl-A-Thon 3000 XL, he was eating the biggest, grossest sandwich that I'd ever seen, and parts of it were falling out of the bun, and he just looked at me.

"I need to use your phone!" I shouted.

"I'm eating lunch," he said.

"It's an emergency!"

He shrugged. "So's lunch."

"Look," I said. *"My dad just got kidnapped in front of your store!"*

"No personal calls," the Ready Player One guy said, and took another bite of his sandwich.

In the digital version of this book—never mind. I don't have time for that now. I wish I did. That way you could actually smell the guy's sandwich drippings and see my face turning red as I wanted to punch him in the nose. I was definitely never going to shop at Ready Player One again, unless they had a game that I absolutely couldn't get anywhere else, or they had one of those exclusive character giveaways. But even then, I wasn't going to like it.

The guy went back to his sandwich. The phone was right there next to him. I reached across the counter to try to get it, but I must have misjudged the distance, because I accidentally knocked his soda over. It spilled everywhere, down the front of the counter and all over the front of my pants.

"Dude, what is your problem?" the Ready Player One guy shouted.

I took a step back and ran into something soft.

That was when I heard the noise behind me.

The noise that you'll be able to hear in the digital version of this book.

It sounded like this:

Twang-twang-twang.

Blunka-blunka-blunka.

[CHAPTER THIRTEEN]

THE RETURN OF THE RETURN OF WESLEY MIDWOOD

I turned around.

Wesley Midwood was standing there behind me. Next to him were Nabeel Sarwani, Rashaad Strong, and Squid Mancini.

"Hey, Pete!" Wesley said. "What's up?" He was holding up a Ready Player One gift card. "Guess what my grandma sent me for my birthday? I'm going to buy Brawl-A-Thon 3000 XL with it. And if there's anything left over—"

"Some guys just kidnapped my dad!" I said.

Wesley stared at me. His mouth was open and his tongue kept swirling around, twanging the rubber bands on his huge teeth. To be honest, it really wasn't helping me figure out what I had to do next. Then his eyes got kind of narrow, and he didn't look like he believed me.

"I thought your dad was playing softball today," Wesley said.

"What's that got to do with it?"

"Yo, man," Rashaad said. "Did you just wet your pants?"

Coke

All three of them were staring at me, where the wet soda stain was spreading over the front of my jeans. The first one to start laughing was Squid.

"He totally did," Nabeel said. "He wet himself!"

"That's Coke," I said. "You can smell it."

They took a big step back, holding their stomachs and whooping at the top of their lungs. Wesley was the only one not laughing. He was probably twanging his braces louder than ever, but I couldn't hear him over the sounds of Nabeel, Squid, and Rasheed completely cracking up.

I looked at the guy behind the counter. "Tell them what happened."

"What can I say?" the Ready Player One guy said, and grinned. "He had an accident."

They all just laughed harder. I turned around and ran outside to my bike. I figured if I could get back home and call Mom on her cell phone, that would probably be my best bet. Maybe there was an explanation behind all of this, like some kind of practical joke.

I got on my bike and started home. Riding with soaking wet sticky jeans wasn't very comfortable, but I tried to ignore it. I kept thinking of heroes from some of the books I'd had to read for school, guys like Johnny Tremain and other characters from history.

I kept thinking about how angry Dad had been about the CommandRoid right before he got kidnapped.

When I got back to the house, Mom's car was parked out on the street. There were a bunch of other cars parked out there too. Mom was standing in the driveway holding my Garage Sale sign, with all kinds of people wandering around looking at the stuff that I'd left out. I realized that I'd forgotten about the whole garage sale thing when I'd gone to Ready Player One.

"Pete," she said, "what is all this? Are you having a garage sale?"

Well, I thought that was kind of obvious. I mean, she had the sign right in her hand. "Mom, I have to tell you something really important!"

"I came home to check on you and saw all this stuff out in our driveway! What were you thinking?"

Before I could answer, Mrs. Wertley came over with Mr. Yappers. She was holding a toaster oven and asked Mom how much she would take for it. Mom told her the toaster wasn't for sale and Mrs. Wertley said that it definitely was, there was a price on it, right here. Mom turned her back on Mrs. Wertley and looked at me.

"What's all over your pants, Pete?" she asked. "Did you have an accident?"

"Mom," I said, "this is really important! Dad's been kidnapped!"

"Don't be ridiculous. Your father's playing softball all day."

She picked up a stack of old clothes that I had draped over the rocking chair in our front yard. "This coat still fits you. Who told you that you could sell any of this?"

"Mom, just listen to me, all right?" I was practically shouting now. "Two guys grabbed Dad and shoved him into the back of a car right out in front of Ready Player One. I just saw it happen!"

"What were you doing at Ready Player One?" Then she looked down and saw that I had Brawl-A-Thon 3000 XL in my hand. "Is that why you were selling all of this? To get money to buy a new game?"

It occurred to me that I wouldn't have had to do any of this if she hadn't borrowed money from my jar, but that probably wasn't the right thing to say right now.

"Mom, please, listen to me, okay?"

But she just told me to go to my room.

"We can talk about this when you've got dry pants on," she said, and at least three people turned and looked up when she said that.

I went inside and headed upstairs to my room.

CHAPTER FOURTEEN

THE BUG MAN
RETURNS

It went something like this:

Okay, that wasn't *exactly* what happened.

This part is true: I was upstairs in my bedroom watching as the Bug Man parked and got out of his van and walked over to my mom. I started taking off my pants, but it took forever to get my legs out. It's hard when your pants are wet.

I opened my pants drawer. It was almost empty. All my pants were dirty, and the only ones left were sweatpants that didn't fit me around the waist. After I managed to get them around my ankles, I looked back out the window for Mom and the Bug Man.

They were both gone.

"Mom!" I ran downstairs, still pulling up my sweatpants, kind of holding them up as I ran, to tell you the truth.

"Pete?" When I got to the entryway, Mom and the Bug Man were in the front hallway. "I thought I asked you to stay in your room."

"Mom," I said, "this is the guy that bought Dad's CommandRoid!" I looked at the Bug Man. "Tell her."

The Bug Man was down on his knees, shining his flashlight into the air vent in the corner. He stood up and stared at me with a funny smile on his face. "Afraid I don't know what you're talking about, sport."

"You were just here an hour ago! You paid me twenty dollars for the CommandRoid game, right before my dad got kidnapped!"

"Kidnapped?" The Bug Man grinned again and turned to my mom with a look like *Kids, can you*

believe it? "I like the imagination. I bet you make your own comic books, don't you?"

"What are you doing back here?" I asked him.

"He was just showing me some of the most common areas for termite infestation in our home," my mom said. She had a pamphlet that the Bug Man had given her.

Mom shivered. "Just the thought of those little horrors crawling around inside these walls is enough to give me nightmares."

"You're not alone, believe you me," the Bug Man said. "I bet you've got a crawlspace in the basement, don't you?"

Mom nodded. "Yes."

The Bug Man turned and pointed his flashlight. "Let's go."

"Mom, wait!"

"Pete, go back to your room."

"But—"

She pointed. *"Now."*

They started to go down into the basement.

Things were desperate. I don't know why I said what I said next. It just slipped out. I yelled:

"MOMMY, NO!"

Mom stopped and stared at me for a second. I felt my face getting really red. But it was too late to take back now. Mom had a really weird look on her face, like she didn't know whether to laugh or take my temperature to see if I had a fever or something.

"'Mommy'?" she said.

"Just . . . call Dad's cell phone, okay?"

Mom must have felt sorry for me a little, because she glanced at the Bug Man. "Excuse me for just a second. This shouldn't take long."

"You take your time," the Bug Man said.

Mom started digging around in her purse for her cell phone. While she was doing that, the Bug Man turned and winked at me and mouthed the word *Mommy* and I felt my whole face getting red all over again. Like *that* guy hadn't ever accidentally called his mother "Mommy" before.

Meanwhile, Mom was still excavating in her

purse, pulling things out and putting them on the little table in the entryway, when her phone started ringing.

"Hello?" Mom said, and smiled. "Oh, hello. How are you? I'm fine, thank you. You know, I've been meaning to call you. I know. I *know*. Well, funny you should mention that, because . . . right. Pete's right here."

I heard a noise behind me and looked around. The Bug Man was gone, but the basement door was open and I could hear him clanking around. The thought of him down there poking around our basement didn't make me feel any better. I turned back to Mom. She was still on the phone, but she was looking at me.

"Really," she said. "No, I didn't know that. Thank you. I will. Oh, he is. Well then, I appreciate that. I will. Okay. Goodbye."

She hung up.

"That was Mrs. Midwood," she said. "Apparently Wesley invited you to a birthday sleepover tonight?"

"Yeah, but—"

"When were you planning on telling me about that?"

"Mom, I don't care about the stupid—"

"Pete, Wesley is your only friend. If you don't

treat him with respect, you're not going to have any friends. Is that what you want?" She didn't wait for me to answer. "Oh, and your father is fine, by the way. Mrs. Midwood said that she just saw him and her husband at the softball game."

"That's not true!" I said. "I saw him get pulled into a car!"

Mom just shook her head. "That's enough. You can finish bringing all those things on the driveway back into the house while I go down to the basement."

"But—"

"Now, mister."

And before I could argue, she went downstairs to meet the Bug Man.

[CHAPTER FIFTEEN]
MORE BAD NEWS

I went back outside. Most of the stuff I'd put out for the garage sale was still sitting where I'd left it. I guess Mom hadn't had much of a chance to put it away before the Bug Man had showed up.

The TV was still plugged in, and somebody must have found a channel that worked, because now there were a bunch of people standing around watching it, but it was just some news broadcast.

The guy on TV was saying that the president had called a special press conference and was going to be coming on in a few minutes. I tried to tell everybody that the garage sale was over, but Mrs. Wertley was there too and she looked pretty interested.

I don't pay very much attention to the news unless it's something really important, like a comet that's about to hit Earth or a snow day at school, so I started picking up the other stuff from the tables.

That was when the president came on. In the digital version of this book, it'll be the actual president, automatically updated to show whoever's in office at the time. But for now this is a guy whose picture I found online.

Then the president did something that I'd never seen him do before:

It was *really* disturbing.

THANK YOU. ANY QUESTIONS?

Nobody knew what to say. I don't think *anybody* had ever seen anything like that before, even Mrs. Wertley, because she had just stood there while the president was making different noises and bugging out his eyes. After a minute the press conference ended.

Mrs. Wertley and everybody else kind of stared at the screen while the reporters tried to figure out what had just happened. I had never watched a press conference before, but I was pretty sure that wasn't how it was supposed to go.

"This is bad," Mrs. Wertley said, "this is really, really bad." Then she turned and hurried away.

Onscreen, the reporters were all trying to figure out what happened. Meanwhile I was trying to put everything together in my mind. Maybe I was going crazy, but it seemed to me that it was all connected somehow.

Anyway, I didn't know what I was going to do about it, even if it was all somehow my fault. Not that I'm saying it was. Crazy things happen all the time with absolutely no explanation except that the world makes no sense. Sometimes I think it would be great if there were one guy who could take responsibility for everything: global warming, soggy french fries, getting picked last at basketball, whatever. It would certainly make things easier—as long as you weren't that guy. Or if you were, they would have to pay you a lot of money. I wouldn't settle for less than twenty million dollars, which is about what Bill Gates made last year. Not a bad deal, considering everyone would blame you for everything.

Then I looked down the driveway at the Bug Man's van.

I realized what I had to do.

[CHAPTER SIXTEEN]
THINGS GET STUPID

Okay. You know that part of the movie where the main character does something incredibly stupid that you would never do in real life, like when the guy says to everybody else that he's going down to find out what that noise was in the basement, and you start yelling at the TV, "Don't go in the basement, you idiot!"?

That's this part.

Except I just have to say that if this ever actually happened to you, you might be surprised by the stupid stuff you'd do.

I walked over to the Bug Man's van. I told myself that it was probably going to be locked, and then I wouldn't even have to worry about it. But when I reached out to the door handle and pulled on it, the door opened right up, and I was staring straight into the passenger seat of the van.

I looked around. There was one of those two-way radios on the dashboard, squawking out static. I saw a cup of coffee and a candy wrapper along with a stack of termite brochures like the one the Bug Man had given Mom, but that was about it.

Then I looked in the back.

The back of the van was a different story. It was full of all kinds of stuff I'd never seen before, like wires and electronic equipment and video screens all hooked up together. It looked like a giant robot had thrown up back there. Or a lot like one of the levels from Brawl-A-Thon 3000, actually.

Not like the stuff you'd use to kill bugs.

I crawled in back. My heart was beating really hard, and I could feel it in my fingertips. I knew this was a bad idea because the Bug Man could come out at any time, and there weren't any windows in the back for me to see him coming. But if there was any chance of finding out what had happened to my dad and the president, I had to at least try.

I started looking around at all the wires and circuit boards and stuff.

Then I saw it, looking dumber and more boring than ever.

The CommandRoid 85.

[CHAPTER SEVENTEEN]

THINGS GET STUPIDER

Yes, it's possible.

In fact, when I publish this book and get famous and go out to school visits, that's going to be the wisdom that I share with America's youth.

REMEMBER, KIDS:
THINGS CAN ALWAYS
GET STUPIDER.

The screen the CommandRoid was attached to was blinking at me. I looked down and saw that there were two joysticks hooked up and everything. The Bug Man knew what he was doing.

I looked at the screen again. In chunky pixelated letters, it said:

I didn't, really, but there didn't seem to be much of a choice. I picked up a joystick and tried to aim the cursor at the box marked YES. The joystick didn't move very well. I didn't get how Dad ever could have used it in the first place, let alone have had fun with it. Finally I got the cursor to where it was supposed to be. Then I pushed the red button.

The screen went black. Then it started filling up with two columns of words that didn't make any sense together. It looked like this:

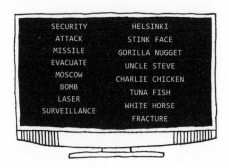

It went on like that for pages and pages, scrolling faster than I could read, but I kept trying to follow it with my eyes anyway. Then something else started happening at the same time. I felt myself getting dizzy, like the whole inside of the Bug Man's van was spinning past me as fast as the words on the screen.

There was something moving back and forth between the two columns. I looked closer and saw that it was a little eight-bit figure.

I stared at the screen until my nose was almost touching it. A voice said:

—HELP ME, PETE!!!!!!

I would have recognized that voice anywhere. *"Dad?"*

[CHAPTER EIGHTEEN]
MY EIGHT-BIT DAD

I just stared at my eight-bit dad. He kept running back and forth between the columns of words. He kept going faster and faster.

"This is awful," he said in a weird digital version of his voice. "This is beyond awful."

"I know," I said. "These graphics stink." My dad's hair looked like a brown brick. His arms and legs seemed to have been built by a kid with a handful of Legos and a short attention span. If it hadn't been for his voice screaming at me for help, I never would have known it was supposed to be him. Then again, what do you expect from an eighties video game?

Meanwhile the columns of words kept scrolling up past him on both sides, faster and faster. From what I could tell, Dad was trying to match up the words on one side of the screen with the different words on the other, but the columns were moving too fast. He was like a guy trying to dodge traffic.

"Help me!" Dad kept saying. "Help me help me helpmehelpmehelpme . . ."

"What do you want me to do?" I shouted, but I didn't think he could hear me. I guess once you've been sucked into a video game or whatever, you can't hear as well, so I tried shouting louder.

"*Dad!* These joysticks are really hard to use! What do you want me to do?"

Dad didn't answer. I stared at the words again. They were blurring now, but I got the weirdest feeling that I was somehow still reading them, trying to put them together in my head, absorbing them faster than I could even realize. I thought of Charlie Chicken. Where had I heard that phrase before? And what about Uncle Steve? My head started pounding and I tried to stop, but my eyes were glued to the screen.

When I looked back at my eight-bit dad, he was staring straight up at the big pile of numbers and words falling down on top of him.

He was screaming.

PETE, DON'T
—— READ THE
CODE WORDS!

"Thanks for telling me now," I mumbled, and felt myself fall forward to the floor of the Bug Man's van, into total blackness.

[CHAPTER NINETEEN]
I GO FOR A LITTLE SPIN

When I opened my eyes, I heard somebody getting into the van.

I sat up fast and instantly regretted it. My skull felt like that level of Brawl-A-Thon 3000 where you have to use your head to punch through a wall of exploding armadillo MechReatures. I glanced at the CommandRoid. The screen in front of me had gone blank.

Up front I could hear the Bug Man climbing into the driver's seat and starting the engine. He wasn't whistling to himself anymore. In fact, from the way he slammed his door, jerked the key in the ignition, and revved the engine, he seemed a lot grouchier than he had earlier. Sometimes in life, I guess, it's not enough to whistle a lot, drive around in a cool van with an insect on top, and call people "sport."

He picked up the two-way radio on the dashboard

and clicked it on. "Hey," he growled, in a voice that didn't sound anything like the one he'd used before. "It's me. The kid's mom let me down into the basement. There's nothing else down there. I think we've got the whole thing."

He twisted his head around and looked back. I ducked my head and froze.

"Yeah," he said, "I've got it here. I hooked it all up. It's running now."

I tried not to move. He hadn't seemed to notice me yet, and I thought if I stayed perfectly still and didn't make a noise, I might have a chance of jumping out the back.

"Okay," the Bug Man said. "I'm headed over now."

Suddenly the van lurched into motion, tires squealing. I grabbed hold of a cabinet on the wall of the van, hoping to keep myself from falling over backwards, but only managed to pull a bunch of loose electronic parts off the shelf next to me. They all fell down with a loud clattering noise, burying me under spools of wire, old circuit boards, and boxes of keyboards and printer cartridges.

"Ow!" I shouted.

The Bug Man slammed on the brakes. He turned around and looked back a second time. I couldn't tell if he'd heard me, but he didn't say anything. My heart was pounding harder than ever, and I could feel drops of sweat running down my back.

He started to come toward the back of the van.

I held my breath. I knew I wasn't going to be able to stay hidden there for more than a few seconds, especially if he started moving things around looking for me. Meanwhile my head was still throbbing from whatever it was I'd seen on that screen before it had finally crushed my dad—if it had really crushed him. After all, it was only the eight-bit version of him. Maybe my real dad was still playing softball. I kind of doubted it, but I try to keep a positive outlook on these things.

I could hear the Bug Man breathing heavily through his mustache. It sounded like a janitor's big push broom sweeping up piles of broken glass and charcoal. One more step and he'd be right on top of me. He reached down and started picking up the stuff that had fallen over.

Then somebody was pounding on the outside of the van.

The Bug Man stopped in his tracks.

"Hello?" a woman's voice was saying from outside, and I heard a dog barking. *"Hello?"*

The Bug Man didn't do anything for a second. He

didn't know who was out there, but I did. I recognized her voice even before I heard her dog barking. It was Mrs. Wertley. The Bug Man started grumbling and went back up to the front of the van. When he opened the door, his voice sounded polite and happy again.

"Well, hello, there, young lady," he said. "What can I do for you?"

"Well, for one thing," Mrs. Wertley snapped, "you can get this giant rolling cockroach out of my neighborhood."

"Giant rolling cockroach?" The Bug Man sounded confused and a little hurt.

"You heard me," Mrs. Wertley said. "I don't know what you think you're doing, but you almost ran over Mr. Yappers, and then you just stopped in the middle of the street."

"But—"

"I don't care to hear your excuses," Mrs. Wertley said, and she slapped the side of the van once more for good measure. *WHAM!* It sounded like she was hitting it with something harder than her hand. It sounded like she was hitting it with a *book*.

"Hey," the Bug Man said. "Stop that!"

Mr. Yappers growled at him.

I saw my chance. The handles of the back doors of the van were right in front of me, and if I jumped up and grabbed them in one quick move, I could escape. I swung myself up, took hold of the door handles, and yanked them as hard as I could.

Except the back doors didn't open.

It turned out there was a very good reason for this.

They were locked.

[CHAPTER TWENTY]

OLD LADY
BLAH-BLAH

I have to stop here for a second and tell you some things that *I really hate* in movies and books:

1) When the hero does something stupid that you would never do, and you don't want him to do it, but he does it anyway. (I already told you this one.)
2) When the bad guy has a change of heart and turns out good in the end. (I **really** hate this and I promise it doesn't happen in this story.)
3) When some annoying little old lady, like somebody's grandma or something, turns out to be tough and funny and helps the hero with something.

I always call that last one "old lady blah-blah," and I can always see it coming a mile away. But I have to warn you: *Right now that's about to happen.*

If I were making up this story, I would leave it out. But since every word here is true, I have to leave it in. So . . .

Sorry!

Anyway, that's when the Bug Man climbed out of the van. "Now, listen," he started.

"No, you listen to me," Mrs. Wertley said, and there was another *WHAM!* as she hit the side of the van. "I'm only going to say this once." *WHAM!* "I don't know what you've got hiding"—*WHAM!*—"in the back of that van"—*WHAM!*—"but before you say another word"—*WHAM!*—"I'd suggest you consider what you say next"—*WHAM!*—"very carefully!"

It was quiet for a long time. When the Bug Man spoke again, his voice sounded different. Softer. But somehow scarier.

"Madam, I'll thank you to stop hitting my vehicle with that large book," he said. "The van belongs to the company, and I'm responsible for any damage."

"For your information," Mrs. Wertley answered, "this book is *Warriner's English Grammar and Composition.* It happens to be the single most important possession that I own."

"That's great," the Bug Man started, "but—"

Mr. Yappers snarled, and I heard the Bug Man

make a sudden loud yelping noise, which I guessed meant Mr. Yappers had bitten him. The Bug Man started saying all kinds of words you can't say in a PG-rated movie, and his voice got farther away, which probably meant that Yappers was chasing him up the street. That gave me a chance to climb forward and hop down into the street, where Mrs. Wertley was waiting with her copy of *Warriner's* still tucked under her arm

She grabbed me by the shoulder.

"Pete, listen to me." Just up the street I could hear Mr. Yappers barking like crazy and snapping and clothes tearing and the Bug Man screaming and trying to get him off, but Mrs. Wertley didn't even seem to notice. In fact, she was just staring straight at me. "Are you listening?"

"Huh?" I said. "Oh. Yeah." Except it turns out that it's really hard to pay attention when somebody is screaming and yelling at a dog less than twenty feet away from you. At least Yappers kept the Bug Man from overhearing what Mrs. Wertley was saying to me.

"Your father is one of the top analysts for the CIA," Mrs. Wertley said. "That CommandRoid game system that you sold at the garage sale is the portal he uses to access the CIA's top-secret database. That means that every government secret is coded inside that system. You have to get it back, do you understand? Right now."

"Wait a second," I stared back at Mrs. Wertley. "Who *are* you?"

"It doesn't matter."

"Is that why the president was talking like that on TV?"

"That's not important right now," she said.

"Why was the president saying 'Wugga-wugga-woo-woo'?" I asked.

Mrs. Wertley sighed. "It's code."

"Wugga-wugga-woo-woo is *code?*" I stared at her. "For *what?*"

"The president was alerting undercover agents around the world by their code names and telling them to go into hiding. Uncle Steve, Banana Pants . . ."

"And Charlie Chicken, too?" I asked.

"Yes, Pete. Charlie Chicken, too." Mrs. Wertley looked very pale. "He was broadcasting information from that list. That data should have never left your father's CommandRoid."

"But I thought my dad worked for Health Solutions Inc.," I said.

"Pete." Mrs. Wertley started shaking me hard enough to make my teeth rattle. "You're not listening

to me. You need to get the CommandRoid back. Think very carefully. Do you have any idea where it might have gone?"

"Well, yeah," I said, pointing at the van. "It's right inside there."

Mrs. Wertley turned and looked around. And right at that moment, the Bug Man finally shook off Mr. Yappers, jumped back into the van, and went squealing away.

CHAPTER TWENTY-ONE

HOW MUCH DO
I STINK?

Mrs. Wertley turned and whistled through her teeth, and Mr. Yappers came running over. He had a little torn-off scrap of the Bug Man's orange uniform in his teeth. Mrs. Wertley took it and pulled out a little plastic bag, sealing it up inside.

"We need to get this to the lab," she said. "They might be able to extract some information from it."

"Are you a spy too?" I asked.

"A field agent, yes." She nodded. "Most retired teachers work for the CIA in one capacity or another."

"*What?*"

"Don't look so shocked. You think we can live on the pension they give us?"

I nodded. "That makes total sense," I said, looking at the book in her arms. "That's why you carry around that copy of *Warriner's English Grammar and Composition,* isn't it? It's actually some kind of computerized weapon or something."

Mrs. Wertley's face became very, very serious. "No, Pete. I carry around *Warriner's* because it is my single most valuable possession. The section on gerunds alone makes it worth owning. I would never dream of going anywhere without it." Before I could answer, she pulled out a cell phone, hitting a speed-dial button. "It's me. We lost the target. He's headed west on Sugarbush Avenue. Yes. I'm told that he still has the CommandRoid." She glared at me. "Are you sure you saw it?"

"Yeah," I said, "definitely, but—"

"Pete, listen to me. Go home and stay there. Lock the door and don't let anyone in. We'll have an agent dispatched to your house immediately."

"Yeah, but—"

"Go."

She was already turning and walking with Mr. Yappers in the opposite direction. I started back up the sidewalk to my house. If my dad was in the CIA and the CommandRoid was the way he accessed the top-secret government database, then what had I done by selling it to the Bug Man for twenty bucks? I thought about the president again, what he'd said on TV. Was I responsible for that, too?

How was I supposed to know my dad was a spy? The most secret thing he'd ever done was replace my goldfish, Luigi, with a new goldfish when Luigi died while I was away at my grandma's house. And he didn't even pick one that *looked* like Luigi.

The only thing that could have been a clue that he was a spy was the way he loves anagrams. He can rearrange letters to make other words faster than anybody I've ever known. Like sometimes he'll look at a sign that says FREE KITTENS, and right away he'll say, "Feet stinker," but it won't be till later that you realize what he did. It's pretty cool, but not exactly spy behavior.

My point is, my dad is not a sneaky guy.

At least that's what I used to think.

I looked at my house. If I went back there, Mom was going to send me straight to my room. And there was someplace else I needed to go first.

It was the last place in the world that I wanted to go.

But the way I saw it, at this point I had no choice.

[CHAPTER TWENTY-TWO]
HELP PETE FIND WESLEY'S HOUSE!

[CHAPTER TWENTY-THREE]

INTO
THE MOUTH
OF MADNESS

I'd already forgotten it was Wesley's birthday. Outside his house there were all these Mario Brothers balloons tied to the mailbox and a big Happy Birthday banner hanging over the front door. Four years ago Wesley's mom bought every Mario Brothers item she could find on eBay, and she's been using them ever since, for every one of his birthdays, even though Wesley and I don't really play that game anymore. I guess they don't make Brawl-A-Thon birthday decorations yet.

Also, Wesley's mom actually used to *call* us the Super Mario Brothers. One time when we went to the grocery store with her, she had us paged on the overhead speakers that way. That was pretty much the end of that.

ATTENTION! WILL THE SUPER MARIO BROTHERS COME MEET PRINCESS MOMMY IN THE CEREAL AISLE?

Anyway, Wesley's mom's van was in the driveway, so that was good. At least he was home. I was out of breath, and the whole way there I'd been looking over my shoulder, expecting the Bug Man's giant cockroach to come rolling around the corner after me. So far, so good.

I rang the bell a couple of times, and Mrs. Midwood opened the door.

"Hi, Mrs. Midwood." I was breathing hard. "Is Wesley home?"

"Yes, he's in the basement. But he said that you weren't coming."

"I really need to see him," I said. "Can I come in?"

"Of course you can, dear." She stepped aside and let me in. "Just take off your shoes."

It had been a while since I'd been to Wesley's

house. I guess I had forgotten how clean it was. Everything in the house was always totally white—the sofa, the chairs, the carpet, the walls—and it seemed like Mrs. Midwood was always running around with a rag, vacuuming or polishing or wiping a thumbprint off the window. She would've been great working in a crime lab.

I walked through the living room, turned toward the basement, and stopped, staring at the blank wall in front of me.

Except . . .

The wall didn't look blank anymore.

Now I was seeing numbers and nonsense words streaming in front of my eyes like the wall was a giant monitor.

CONVENTION	GORILLA
AIRPORT	SEAGULL
FREEWAY	WOLF
CENTER	NUGGET
MALL	POODLE
FACTORY	DUCK
BUNKER	SAUCE
HOSPITAL	BISHOP
COMPUTER	DRIVE
POWER	INCHWORM
STATION	GOLDFISH
SHELTER	TORTOISE
MISSILE	PYTHON
SILO	MOLE
LIBRARY	HOLE
	SQUID

It just kept going and going like that. After a second I realized this was all the stuff I'd seen in the Bug Man's van. All the information that Dad had told me not to look at. Except now *it was stuck in my head.* Like it was behind my eyes somewhere. Maybe it was seeing all that blinding white, or the fact that I'd run over here as fast as I could, but all of a sudden I felt really dizzy, like I was about to pass out.

"Are you okay, Peter?" Mrs. Midwood asked. "You look so white."

My first thought was: *How can she tell, with all this white everywhere?*

My second thought was: *She's right.*

My third thought was: *THUD.*

I hit the floor.

Then I blacked out.

CHAPTER TWENTY-FOUR

WHERE BABIES
DON'T COME FROM
OR, HOW I RUINED
EVERYTHING (AGAIN)

When I opened my eyes this time, Mrs. Midwood was staring down at me, looking really worried. I hardly noticed. Because standing right next to her was the most beautiful girl I'd ever seen.

She looked like a redheaded angel with red lips, and I remembered her from before.

The words spilled off my lips before I could stop them.

HELLO, MY ANGEL.
WHAT SHADE OF LIPSTICK
ARE YOU WEARING?

Callie Midwood frowned down at me. Seeing her frown made me realize where I was, and who she was, and what I'd just said to her. It hit me like a fork in an electrical outlet. I tried to sit up, but I guess I sat up too fast, because the top of my head smacked her in the mouth.

"Ow!" she shouted, pulling back and putting her hand up to her face. "You just split my lip!"

I got up and ran downstairs. The last thing I heard was Callie asking her mom for some ice to put on her lip.

Down in the basement, Wesley was sitting with Nabeel, Squid, and Rashaad, surrounded by bowls of chips and bottles of soda and playing the brand-new **BRAWL-A-THON 3000 XL** on Wesley's sixty-inch flat-screen TV with the volume turned up to a chest-vibrating level.

And, okay, I'm not going to lie to you. *It looked amazing.*

I mean, the graphics were awesome. The creatures were bigger and more fierce than anything I'd ever been up against. The sound effects were crunchier, somehow. (In the digital version of this book, you'll be able to hear them in Dolby THX. In fact, by the time the digital version of this book is available, the publishers will probably have installed a version of the game itself right here in the middle so if you wanted to, you could just stop reading, click on GO, and play as long as you wanted before you went back to reading the next chapter. I'm always thinking about stuff like this—I'm way ahead of my time.)

For now, though, I'll just say this. Even with everything else that was going on—Dad being a spy, the president talking crazy on TV, me smacking Callie Midwood in the mouth with my head—all I could do for a moment was stand there and bask in the awesomeness.

"Oh, hey, Pete," Wesley said. "What's up?"

I couldn't take my eyes off the screen. "Is this it?"

"Yeah," he said. "Cool, huh?"

"It looks amazing."

"Wanna play?"

"Totally." I started to sit down, then remembered why I was there. "Wait, no. Wesley, I have to talk to you."

"Sure," he said. "Just let me finish this level."

"Dude," Nabeel shouted, "look out for Electric Shoctopus!"

I watched as Wesley frantically tried to shovel a bunch of machine parts into this giant half-constructed grizzly bear MechReature he was building before the ten-thousand-volt octopus could wrap its electric cables around the bear's throat. Wesley's mouth was open and his tongue was twanging his rubber bands like crazy and the clock was ticking and I could already see there was no way he was going to make it. I grabbed the controller from Rasheed and started helping him put the different pieces together.

"Hey!" Rashaad said. "What's the big idea?"

I turned to the screen.

This was my turf. I might not be able to run a garage sale or track down the Bug Man, but this was something I knew how to handle.

I CAN DO THIS.

All of a sudden everything froze. The different pieces of the grizzly MechReature started floating back out and flying across the screen. Now there were two extra Rashaads doing the exact opposite of what I was trying to get the first Rashaad to do.

"What's happening?" I asked.

"Time is going sideways," Nabeel said. "It does that."

"Oh, man, I totally forgot about that!"

"Uh-huh. Tried to warn you. You have to stay out of your own way or you'll annihilate yourself."

I tried to move, but one of the other versions of Rashaad kept doing the exact opposite, and the other kept doing and undoing what I was working on. I noticed a creepy black circle forming around the three versions of Rashaad as I worked. Meanwhile Wesley was eating Doritos and twanging the rubber bands on his teeth faster than ever. Little orange crumbs were flying everywhere.

"What am I supposed to do?" I shouted.

"Break the cycle!" Squid yelled.

"I don't know what that means!"

"You have to break the cycle before time loops around you!" Nabeel shouted.

"What happens if I fail?"

"Then events from Rashaad's past keep happening around us endlessly!" Wesley shouted.

I sat forward, gripping the controller in both hands, sweat popping out along my upper lip. I finished building the grizzly MechReature, but it was too late. The time loop sealed around us. Wesley tried to use the bear's chainsaw claws to slash the loop open, but it just kept getting tighter.

"Arrrrggh!" Wesley shouted. *"Can't breathe!"*

"Hold on," I said. "I want to try something." And before any of them could stop me, I took hold of the grizzly MechReature I'd just built, and I started tearing it apart.

"What are you doing?" Wesley shouted.

"Dude," Nabeel said, "give it up. You're doomed."

"Not yet." I started tearing everything else apart too, destroying all the creations that everybody else had built, not just the creatures but the environment itself. And the game was letting me do it.

"Pete," Wesley said, "are you *nuts?*"

"Time can go backwards, right?"

"Yeah, but that only happens when the game wants it to."

"What if we *make* it go backwards?"

"What, like, on *purpose?*" Squid asked. "That's crazy! Why—?"

Then he stopped.

It was working. Everything onscreen *was* going backwards. Time itself had reversed its flow. The black circle of the time loop started spinning in the other direction until it tore itself apart completely, clearing the entire screen, and a big word bubble popped up:

!SNOITALUTARGNOC

"Huh?" Rashaad said, and the word reversed itself:

CONGRATULATIONS!

We all slumped back with a gasp of relief.

"Whoa, Pete, that was awesome!" Wesley had landed in a bowl of Doritos, and he was picking chips out of his hair. "How did you know it was going to do that?"

"Just a guess," I said, except that wasn't exactly true. The fact was that I'd kind of stolen the idea from *Superman: The Movie,* which came out way back in the seventies. My dad made me watch it with him one afternoon when there wasn't anything else to do. It was a pretty corny movie in a lot of ways, but the end, when . . .

SPOILER ALERT!!!!

. . . Lois Lane dies and Superman brings her back to life and saves the world by flying around the whole planet backwards, faster and faster, until he reverses the earth's rotation and makes time go backwards, was pretty cool.

······································

END SPOILER ALERT!!!

······································

Wesley was still looking at the video game screen. "That was the coolest," he said.

"Thanks," I said, and tossed a handful of Doritos in my mouth. I was feeling pretty good about it myself.

"What did you have to tell me about again?" Wesley asked.

"Huh?" I glanced at him. "Oh yeah." I looked back at Squid, Rashaad, and Nabeel. "Is there someplace private we can talk?"

I was already starting to walk back toward the corner of the basement, but Wesley hadn't moved. He had this funny look on his face I'd never seen before.

"Come on," I said. "What's your problem?"

"Mom said we're not best friends anymore," Wesley said.

I frowned at him. "What?"

"She said you took advantage of our friendship."

"Come on," I said. "That's ridiculous. What did I do?"

"Like when you spread that rumor that I had a contagious skin rash all over my back that was shaped like the state of Texas," Wesley said.

"I didn't spread that rumor," I said. All I'd told everybody was that I'd *heard* Wesley had a skin rash, and that it *might* be contagious, and that it *could* have been shaped like Texas, which wasn't even remotely the same thing, and the only reason I'd done it was so that I wouldn't have to come over to his house and risk making some awkward scene with Callie. "Come on, this is serious."

"Anything you can say to Wesley, you can say to us," Nabeel said.

"Yeah, we're his friends now," Squid said. Without taking his eyes off the screen, he picked up the Doritos bag and shook the last crumbs into his mouth, then crumpled it up and tossed it on the floor. "Yo, Doublewide, you got any more Cool Ranch? This bag's empty."

"Sure, I think," Wesley said.

"Well, what are you waiting for?" Nabeel asked.

"Yeah," Rashaad said. "Hop to it."

"Okay. I'll be right back." Wesley jumped for the stairs. I followed him.

"Wesley," I said, "those guys aren't your friends."

Wesley peered at me suspiciously. "How would you know?"

"Just trust me, okay?"

"They treat me better than—"

"Yo, Mount Flabmore!" Nabeel shouted up from below. "Bring down another two-liter of Mountain Dew while you're at it!"

I looked at him. "You were saying?"

"That's just how we talk to each other. He calls me Mount Flabmore, and I call him . . . Nabeel."

"Because that's his name."

Wesley twanged his rubber bands, and his eyes shifted away uneasily. "Well, yeah, but . . ."

"Look," I said, "it's not up to me, so I don't care who you hang out with. That's not why I came here anyway."

"It's not?" Now he looked disappointed. "But I thought—"

"No," I said. "Listen. Remember at the garage sale this morning, when you saw that CommandRoid and you said that your dad had one of them too?"

"Yeah. I mean, I guess."

"Where is it?"

"Up in his study. But I'm not allowed to go up there." Wesley's face turned a little pinker, and he lowered his voice. "He only let me in there one time last year, to talk to me about where babies come from."

I shuddered. I remembered Wesley coming to school the next day and telling everybody what his father had said about where babies come from. I'm not sure what his dad said originally, but if you broke it all down into a pie chart, Wesley's version of it would look something like this:

Where Babies Come From (according to Wesley)

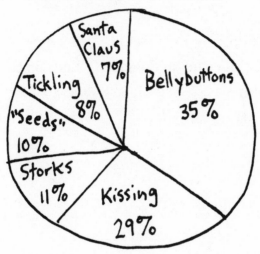

Anyway, one thing was for sure: Wesley's dad hadn't done him any favors in the popularity department. There were kids who still weren't talking to him because of that.

"Yo, Chunk Muffin!" Rashaad yelled up the stairs. "We got any kind of ETA on those Doritos?"

"Coming right up!" Wesley yelped, and I saw him getting nervous. "I can't go in there right now, Pete," he said. "I've got guests."

"Wesley," I said, "this is important."

"Yeah, but—"

I took a deep breath, knowing what I was going to have to say. "It's time for the Super Mario Brothers to get back together."

Wesley looked at me for a long time. "You seriously mean it?"

"Uh-huh."

"Okay," he said, and nodded. "Let's do this thing."

[CHAPTER TWENTY-FIVE]
WE DO THIS THING

The first thing we had to do was get the key to Wesley's dad's study. That wasn't too hard, because he kept a spare hanging in the laundry room, on a key chain that said DAD'S STUDY. It was a big brass key that looked old and heavy, like if you hit somebody with it, you could put them in the hospital.

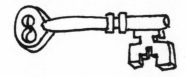

"Whoa," I said. "That's some key."

"We have to be quiet," Wesley said. "Mom's polishing the silver in the dining room and—"

"*Wesley?* Where are you going with that key to your father's study?"

His mom's head popped around the corner. I considered running for it, but that wouldn't have done much good. Fortunately, at that moment Nabeel came bursting up from the basement with the empty chip bowl in both hands.

"Yo, Blubber Nuggets! We got a serious chip short-age down here, and—" He stopped when he saw Mrs. Midwood looking at him. "Oh, hey, Wesley's mom."

Mrs. Midwood's eyes got huge. *"Blubber Nuggets?"*

I glanced at Wesley, and I could tell we were both thinking the same thing. Mrs. Midwood hated it when anybody made fun of Wesley's weight. It had been a sore spot since kindergarten, and I'm pretty sure that it bothered her even more than it bothered him. She'd been to the principal's office four times, and on the fourth time she'd brought a lawyer with her.

She was still inhaling a breath to unload on Na-beel when Wesley and I spun around the corner and started upstairs with the key. His dad's study was at the end of the hallway, and when we got there, I stepped back while Wesley put the key in the lock.

"This place makes me think of storks and seeds," he said.

The lock went *click* and we stepped inside.

His dad's study was this big dark room with book-shelves on the walls and a giant wooden desk in front of the window. It smelled like old paper and leather furniture. Wesley turned on the light, and I saw it sit-ting there on the desk.

The CommandRoid in all its glory.

Just like Dad's.

It was hooked up to a TV set with the joysticks sitting out on either side.

"Well, what are you waiting for?" I said. "Switch it on."

Wesley hit the power button and turned on the TV. The screen lit up with chunky pixelated letters:

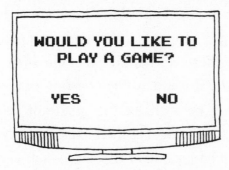

"What am I supposed to say?" Wesley asked.

"Click YES." I already had a joystick in my hand. Wesley picked up the other one. This controller felt like it was carved out of wood. It was so unresponsive that I wondered if it was hooked up at all. Now I knew how the pioneers had felt when they'd played video games while crossing the prairie back in the eighteen hundreds or whatever.

"Ugh," Wesley said. "I can barely budge it."

"Push harder," I told him. "You can do it."

"I'm trying!" Wesley said. "Oh, man. This is really hard!" He released the joystick and shook his hand out. "My fingers are going numb!" He glanced at me. "What about yours?"

"Mine doesn't work at all. Here, trade me." I reached over and took Wesley's joystick, grabbed the top part, and shoved it forward. The cursor moved a little. I pushed harder.

CRACK!

I guess maybe I shouldn't have done that.

The top of the controller had snapped off in my hand. Now there were a bunch of old wires that were never meant to see the light of day dangling out of the bottom. The sight of the inside of broken video games makes me feel a little sick, like I've accidentally stumbled on one of those medical shows where they show surgical procedures.

Wesley's face went totally white. His mouth became a perfect O of sheer terror.

"You broke Dad's game," he said. "I'm so dead!"

"Okay, just calm down; it's going to be okay. We can fix it." I tried to push the top part of the controller back into place, but it wouldn't fit.

"Wesley?" his mom's voice cried from downstairs, getting louder, and I heard the *thump-thump-THUMP* of her feet up the steps. "What are you doing?"

"Dude," Wesley said, "whatever you're going to do, hurry up!"

What was I supposed to do? I mean, if this were a choose-your-own-adventure story, this would be one of those moments when . . .

A) If you want Pete to shove the two parts of the joystick together and try to convince Mrs. Midwood it still works, turn to page 79.

B) If you want Pete to jump out the window and try not to break his leg when he hits the ground, turn to page 193.

Except I hate those kind of stories, because I always end up dead, eaten by a shark or lost at sea or something, and anyway I haven't even written page 193 yet. How am I supposed to know what happens?

How am I supposed to know if there's even going to be a page 193? I could be dead in five seconds.

Meanwhile Wesley pointed at the screen, where two columns of digitized code words had scrolled up again like the walls of a prison.

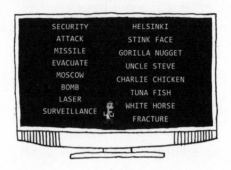

In between the walls, a tiny eight-bit figure was running back and forth, frantically carrying words from one column to the other and back again. But every time he moved a word, another one just slid up to take its place.

Wesley grunted. He was still trying to control the action with his own joystick.

"What is that thing?" he shouted.

"That's my dad," I mumbled.

The footsteps on the stairs got louder.

"My mom's coming!" Wesley said. "We have to hide this! We're so dead! If she tells my dad about what happened—"

It was too late. A figure stepped into the doorway.

"What are you two doing?" a voice asked.

I turned around.

It wasn't Mrs. Midwood.

It was Callie.

[CHAPTER TWENTY-SIX]

KNOCK-KNOCK.
WHO'S THERE?
INTERRUPTING END
OF THE WORLD.
INTERRUPTING END
OF THE WORLD WH—?
BOOM!

I know: dumb name for a chapter. But it *felt* like the end of the world, me standing there with a broken joystick in my hand while Callie Midwood stared at both of us with her green eyes, holding a bag of frozen peas against her swollen lip.

She had never looked more beautiful.

"We're just trying to . . ." I said, and the words just kind of floated away. It seemed like a good start, but unfortunately I didn't know where to go from there. It felt like there was an invisible elephant standing on my chest, squashing all the air out of my lungs.

Callie's eyes danced from the broken joystick to

the CommandRoid, the text and numbers scrolling over the screen, and back to us. She slowly lowered the bag of peas from her lip.

"Dad is going to kill you," she said.

"I know!" Wesley said. His sister had just said the words that he feared the most, and he suddenly seemed to have to go to the bathroom very badly. He was shifting from one foot to the other, his face white with panic. "I know! I know!"

"Ugh." Callie sighed. "Follow me."

Before either of us could ask questions, she grabbed us and pulled us out of Mr. Midwood's study, swinging us around the corner to safety just as Wesley's mom came down the hall. I heard Mrs. Midwood say Wesley's name again as Callie whisked us through another doorway, shut the door, turned, and looked at us.

"We were just—" Wesley started.

"Shut up," she whispered. "Don't even breathe."

There was a knock. "Callie?" Mrs. Midwood asked from the hallway.

"What?" Callie shouted.

"Have you seen Wesley and Pete?"

Callie glared at us. "No," she said. "Aren't they in Jerk Face's room?"

"They most certainly are not," Mrs. Midwood said. "They were in your father's study, but they aren't there now."

"How should I know where they are?"

"I'm simply asking for a little help, Callie," Mrs. Midwood said. "Are you sure you didn't—"

"Maybe they climbed out onto the roof and fell off," Callie said. "If we're lucky."

Mrs. Midwood was silent for a minute. I imagined her standing out there in the hallway with one of those cartoon storm clouds over her head while she tried to decide what to do. Then finally, after what felt like forever, I heard her footsteps go thumping away.

I let out a sigh of relief and looked up at Callie. "Thank y—"

"Shut up," she said. "My mouth still hurts where you head-butted me."

"And I'm really sorry about th—"

"Shut up."

"Okay."

"And stop staring at me."

I nodded and stared at my shoes. Wesley stood next to me. He didn't seem to have to go to the bathroom anymore, but he didn't look too happy about things either. In the awkward silence I looked around the bedroom. Callie's walls were pale pink like the inside of a seashell, and it smelled like perfume and hair product, and there were piles of clothing on the floor. The little TV on her dresser was turned to CNN. Posters hung on the wall, pictures of musicians I'd never heard of with names like Beth Orton and the Mountain Goats and the Killers and Taken by Trees. I tried to memorize as many of the names as I could in case Callie and I ever went out on a date.

I forgot that we weren't supposed to talk.

"You know," I said, "it was really cool of you to—"

"What part of 'shut up' do you not understand?" Callie asked, but she must have thought we didn't understand what it meant at all, because then she asked: "What were you two doing in Dad's study with that stupid video game anyway?"

But then she wasn't even looking at us anymore. She was staring at the TV, where the words I'd come to fear the most were popping up onscreen: *SPECIAL BULLETIN*. The anchorwoman was saying that in a few minutes the president was going to address the nation again.

"This should be good," she said.

"I know," I said, and this time she didn't bother telling me to shut up.

Then the president came on.

MY FELLOW AMERICANS . . .

As I stared at the president on TV, I felt something happening inside my brain. I don't know how to describe it. *I knew what he was going to say.*

I started talking just before he did.

I PUT BIRD POOP IN MY HAIR.

I PUT BIRD POOP IN MY HAIR.

I HAVE TO SAY
I LIKE IT THERE.

I HAVE TO SAY I LIKE IT THERE.

MORE THAN IN
MY UNDERWEAR.

MORE THAN IN MY UNDERWEAR.
THANK YOU. ANY QUESTIONS?

When the president finished, Callie and Wesley were both staring at me.

"How did you know what he was going to say?" Callie asked.

"I know a lot more than that," I said.

"What does it mean?"

"It's in my head," I said.

"What?" Wesley twanged his rubber bands. "The bird poop?"

"The code," I said. "That's why my dad told me not to read the words off the CommandRoid's display. That's why the Bug Man wanted it. Now all the codes are in my brain. I can't get them out."

"Pete." Callie blinked at me slowly. "Would it bother you too much," she asked, "if I told you that I have *absolutely no idea* what you're talking about?"

"It's okay," I said. But it wasn't. My skull was starting to ache and throb again, worse than ever. "That's actually good that you don't understand, because if you knew, then it would mean that it was in your head too, and . . ."

I stopped talking. Onscreen, the president's advisors were leading him from the podium while reporters shouted questions at him from the crowd. He was still talking. I felt the words and numbers coming together in my brain, but they weren't linking up quite right.

"It's a warning," I said.

"Of what?" Callie asked. "What's going to happen?"

"Some kind of attack." I shut my eyes. The words scrolled by at the speed of light, phrases that I couldn't understand. "Bird poop. In his hair. Uncle

Steve. Banana Pants. Underwear . . . I don't know; it's all so blurry."

"Try," Callie said.

I just stood there. The details were like a slippery piece of soap that I couldn't get a grip on, and the harder I tried, the faster it squirted out of my grasp. I hate that kind of soap. "I need to get back to the CommandRoid. It's the only way of getting the facts out of my head."

"Too bad you broke it," Callie said.

"What, your head?" Wesley asked.

"The CommandRoid," I said.

"Wait," Wesley said. He stared at me. "So the secret codes are stuck in your brain?"

"That's what I've been trying to tell you," I said. "Yes."

Then Wesley said something that I'd never heard him say before:

"I have a plan."

CHAPTER TWENTY-SEVEN

WESLEY'S NOT-SO-AWESOME PLAN OF NOT-SO-AWESOMENESS

Remember back in chapter 8 when Wesley said that Squid Mancini could hypnotize people?

Well, neither do I.

But apparently Wesley did, because that was all part of his plan. (In the digital version of this book, you'll hear theme music playing here.)

THE PLAN

While Callie distracted Mrs. Midwood by telling her that she'd just noticed a weird stain on the living room carpet, Wesley and I snuck back down to the basement, where Squid, Nabeel, and Rashaad were still playing Brawl-A-Thon 3000 XL on the flat-screen plasma TV.

In other words, not much had changed in that department.

"Yo, Flab Apples," Nabeel said, without taking his eyes off the screen, "you bring those Doritos down yet?"

Wesley looked embarrassed, and I poked him with my elbow.

"Guys," Wesley said, "we need your help."

"What, you mean like help *eating Doritos?*" Rashaad asked. He was on some level that I'd never seen before, which wasn't surprising because I'd hardly played this new version of the game. "Because I can definitely help you with that."

"Let me just finish this tarantula MechReature," Squid said, his fingers flying frantically across the controller. "I'm almost there. Come to papa."

"Dude, look behind you!" Nabeel said.

"Where?" Squid said.

"Right behind you! Look out!"

All at once the screen went blank. Squid looked behind him, where Callie was standing with the plug in her hand.

"Now," she said, "are you little dweebs ready to help?"

• • •

"I can't really hypnotize people, you know," Squid muttered, when we explained the plan to him. "I just had to do a report on it last year for school."

"So you must know *something* about it then," Callie said.

Squid shrugged. "I kind of wrote it at the last minute," he said.

"Forget it," I said. "This isn't going to work."

"We have to try," Wesley said.

"I don't even get how hypnotizing me is supposed to help."

"Okay, look." Wesley gave me this exasperated look, which I didn't appreciate, considering he was the one who still came to school with a Lorax lunchbox full of Yu-Gi-Oh! cards. "You've got all this information in your head, right? Only it's all, like, stuck up there where you can't get to it—kind of like when I stuff too many pairs of underwear in my drawer and I can't get it open." He pointed at my skull. "If we hypnotize you, it might help get all that underwear out."

Right away I was pretty sure it was a bad idea. The only person I'd ever seen hypnotized was in a YouTube video where a guy volunteered to go onstage at a nightclub, and the hypnotist convinced him that he had a live chicken in his pants. Wesley and I had watched it and laughed our butts off, but all of a sudden it didn't seem so funny.

"I don't know," I said, and then I saw Callie staring at me with a different look in her eyes.

"I can't believe I'm saying this," she said, "but my brother might be kind of right."

"Fine," Squid said, "but if I'm going to do this, I'm going to need some kind of shiny object, like a coin or something. Anybody got anything like that?"

"Here." Callie took off her necklace and handed it to Squid. "Try this."

Squid looked at the pendant on Callie's necklace. It was a gold locket on a chain. I wondered where she'd gotten it, if her boyfriend had given it to her or whatever, if she even had a boyfriend. Finally he shrugged. "This'll work."

Meanwhile Nabeel was getting out his iPhone.

"What are you doing?" Callie asked.

"If you're going to hypnotize Pete," Nabeel said,

"I want to record this, just in case he does something cool."

"Okay," Squid said, turning to me. "I want you to relax and watch this necklace. Just watch it, and listen to my voice." He held Callie's locket in front of my face, swinging it back and forth. "I'm going to count backwards from twenty. Nineteen ... eighteen ... seventeen ... sixteen ..."

"This is taking too long," I said.

"You have to give it a chance," Wesley said.

I glanced at Callie. "Just don't let them convince me I've got a chicken in my pants, okay?"

"Pete," Wesley said, "trust us, okay?"

" ... twelve ... eleven ... ten ..."

I shook my head. "This is so not going to work."

It was the last thing I remember saying.

[CHAPTER TWENTY-EIGHT]
THE GREAT AWAKENING

I woke up to the sound of people screaming. At least that's what I thought. It turns out that when people are laughing hard enough, it sounds like screaming.

I was standing in the middle of the basement. Something was wrong.

I felt strangely cold.

All around me Nabeel, Squid, and Rashaad were laughing so hard that they could hardly breathe. Wesley wasn't looking at me—he was staring at the iPhone in his hand. Callie was nowhere to be seen.

I spun around. My clothes were lying in a pile in the corner, next to the game console and an empty Doritos bag.

I grabbed them and started trying to pull on my sweatpants, but my foot got caught and I fell against the back wall while I yanked the pant leg up. By the time I got my shirt on, Wesley was looking at me too. I couldn't believe it.

"How could you let them do this to me?" I shouted.

"Pete, wait," Wesley said. "I can explain!" He tried to say something else, but I didn't hear it over the laughter.

I ran upstairs out of the basement and out the front door.

"Callie!" Mrs. Midwood said behind me. "I still don't see that stain!"

I slammed the door and ran.

[CHAPTER TWENTY-NINE]
THE CRACK-UP

I was running so fast that I almost got hit by the car pulling into Wesley's driveway. It was Wesley's dad, Mr. Midwood. He was still wearing his company softball team uniform. Their team was the Health Solutions Inc. Badgers.

"Afternoon, Pete," he said, "is everything okay?"

"No," I said, and standing there in the driveway I let it all come spilling out—about my dad getting kidnapped and the Bug Man and the CommandRoid putting all those numbers and code words in my head. I didn't tell him that I broke the joystick on his CommandRoid up in his study. Well, I sort of did. "And the worst part is, Mr. Midwood, Wesley broke your joystick."

Mr. Midwood listened to all of this quietly. He didn't even get mad. When I was finished, he reached down and patted me on the shoulder. "It's all right, Pete. Your dad's fine."

"He is?"

"Sure, he's right in the car with me. I brought him back from the softball game just now. See?"

I ran over to the guy in the baseball cap who was sitting in the passenger seat of Mr. Midwood's car. "Dad?"

The door opened, but the guy in the passenger seat wasn't my father.

It was the Bug Man.

"Hey, kid," the Bug Man said, unbuckling his seat belt and climbing out. "Wanna see what your friend's dog did to my uniform?"

It was the most horrible thing I'd ever seen. I looked back at Mr. Midwood, but he didn't look friendly anymore. He'd taken off his baseball cap, and he wasn't smiling.

"Get in the car, Pete."

"What . . . ?" I stared at him. "What about my dad?"

"I said, get in the car."

"Wait," I said. "You . . . you're . . ."

The Bug Man grabbed me and tossed me in the back. Then he jumped into the passenger seat next to Wesley's dad. As Mr. Midwood pulled out of the driveway, I saw Wesley come flying out of the house, waving.

"Dad!" he was shouting. "Did you remember to pick up the cake?" Then he stopped with a confused look on his face. "Wait, where are you going?"

In the back seat, I tried to sit up and shout to Wesley that his dad was working with the Bug Man, but the Bug Man turned around and shoved me down, covering my mouth with a stinky old T-shirt. Up in the driver's seat Mr. Midwood yelled, "I'm just going to pick up a couple quarts of ice cream, son. I'll be right back!"

"Cool!" Wesley shouted. "Get vanilla bean!"

Wesley, no, I thought, but I couldn't say anything as the car peeled out of the driveway and spun away.

"What an idiot," Mr. Midwood mumbled as he drove. That was when I knew he wasn't a good dad. You're not supposed to say that stuff out loud.

"You can let him up now," he told the Bug Man, and I saw Mr. Midwood's eyes glaring back at me from the rearview mirror.

"You know what irritates me, Pete?" he said. "I mean, more than the fact that you messed up three years of work trying to steal those codes from your father?"

"No," I said.

"Those were *my* x-ray specs that you were selling at your garage sale. I've had them since I was a kid. Wesley borrowed them and then he left them at your house, and then you actually tried to sell them back to him."

"Wait," I said. "You mean all of this is about a pair of x-ray specs?"

"Don't be a moron," Mr. Midwood said. "It's about the government codes on that CommandRoid that I'm going to use to humiliate the president and topple the government and eventually take over the world. But . . ." He paused. "The whole thing with the x-ray specs didn't help. Fortunately for you . . ."

I looked back at the rearview mirror.

I HAVE ANOTHER PAIR!

I almost screamed. It was pretty hideous.

"Never mess with another man's x-ray specs," Mr. Midwood said.

"Wait a second." The Bug Man looked at me. "Is your T-shirt on backwards?"

"At least I'm not the one with the hole in his pants," I said.

"Shut up, both of you," Mr. Midwood snapped. He'd taken the x-ray specs off for now, at least. That was a relief. It helped me think clearly again.

"If you don't have my father, then where is he?" I asked.

"Funny you should ask," Mr. Midwood said. "We're going to see him right now."

[CHAPTER THIRTY]

IN THE LAIR OF THE BUG MAN

Mr. Midwood pulled up in front of what looked like an abandoned warehouse with a big sign out in front that said BUGGED? CALL THE BUG MAN. Apparently this was his headquarters. There weren't any other Bug Man cars in front of it, though.

Just the Bug Man's red van.

"Get out," Mr. Midwood said.

"Hold on," I said. "First explain to me what's going on here. Aren't you my dad's boss at Health Solutions Inc.?"

Mr. Midwood let out a big sigh.

"Health Solutions Inc. is a fake business, Pete. Okay? You think I know anything about health care?"

"But then—"

"I started it for the same reason I bought a CommandRoid for myself—so I could steal the codes from your father. I always knew he was a data analyst

123

for the CIA. Unfortunately, even since I had him kidnapped, he hasn't done me any good sorting out those codes. I got some of them, which was why the president came on TV and started warning all the undercover agents around the world about what was happening. But that was only one percent of what's stored on the CommandRoid. That's why I had to insert your dipstick of a father into the program to get the rest of them." He pointed to the Bug Man's van. "Let's see how he's doing with it."

We opened the rear door of the van and climbed in. It was a pretty tight fit with me and the Bug Man and Mr. Midwood all squeezed in there without much fresh air, and I kind of started wishing that the Bug Man had changed into another pair of pants.

Anyway, Dad's CommandRoid was still there, but when I looked at the screen, all I saw were code words streaming across it. "Where's my dad?" I asked.

Mr. Midwood looked at the Bug Man, and the Bug Man shrugged.

"He was in there last time I looked."

"Wait," I said. "You shrank my dad down and inserted him into this lame video game to help you translate the codes, and now you lost him in there?"

Mr. Midwood grinned. It was not the grin of a healthy man. "You know what?" he said. "I can think of at least one way to find him and get him back." He turned to the Bug Man. "Go ahead."

The Bug Man picked up something from the floor of the van that I hadn't seen before. It looked like a giant blow dryer with a bunch of wires and tubes attached to the sides and cords plugged into the machine in the back. But the weird thing was, it wasn't scary.

Not so much this.   More like this.

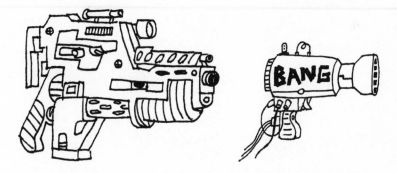

I couldn't help it. I started laughing. Maybe it was just nerves, or everything I'd just been through, but he was threatening me with a hair dryer with the word *BANG* written on the side in black duct tape.

"This isn't funny," Mr. Midwood said. "You think this is funny? Once I shoot you with the digitizer and you're trapped inside the game with your father, then we'll see who's laughing."

"Digitizer?" I kept laughing. Tears were squirting

from my eyes and trickling down my cheeks. "How long did it take you write the word 'BANG' on the side?" I asked.

"That's for me to know and you to find out," Mr. Midwood said. He turned to the Bug Man and nodded at the digitizer. "Get him, Stanley."

"Stanley?" I looked at the Bug Man. "Your name's *Stanley?*"

"It's a family name," the Bug Man said, and pulled the trigger.

[CHAPTER THIRTY-ONE]
BANG!

It wasn't the sound of the digitizer shrinking me down and putting me into the CommandRoid 85. It was the sound of somebody crashing into the back of Stanley the Bug Man's van.

We all fell to the floor. Stanley the Bug Man landed with his butt sticking up in the air, and I don't want to tell you where I landed. Let's just say I didn't stay there long. The crazy blow dryer of doom hit the floor. Mr. Midwood shouted, "What's happening?"

I pushed open the back door of the van and saw the purple car right behind us. Behind the wheel sat Callie Midwood. She was staring at me through the windshield. Wesley was in the passenger seat. He gaped, slack-jawed, at his father next to the Bug Man in the back of the van. The Bug Man was bent over trying to pick up the parts of the equipment that had fallen everywhere during the collision. You don't really need to see a picture of that, do you? Good.

Wesley and Callie looked like they wished they'd never come.

"Dad?" Callie said.

"You said you were going for vanilla bean!" Wesley shouted out the window. "You lied!"

I jumped out of the van and climbed into the back of Callie's car.

Callie put it in reverse, swung around, and floored it.

"How did you find me?" I asked.

"Pete." Wesley turned around and handed me Nabeel's iPhone. "I think you better take a look at this," he said.

I looked down and saw my face looking back at me from the phone's screen.

"What is this?"

"This is what happened when Squid hypnotized you," Wesley said. "You don't remember anything you said when you were hypnotized, do you?"

I shook my head. "Show me."

"You sure?"

"Positive."

Wesley held up the iPhone and hit PLAY.

CHAPTER THIRTY-TWO

WHAT THE IPHONE SAID

OKAY, I JUST HAVE TO SAY . . .

"Wow," I said. "I guess Squid knew what he was doing after all."

My eyes were riveted to the screen. I didn't remember saying any of the words that were coming out of my mouth. But I was still talking.

STINK FACE GORILLA NUGGET

"Stink face gorilla nugget?" Callie said.

"Yeah. I think it means . . ." I paused. "There's going to be some kind of attack at the convention center today at four o'clock." I started to hand him back the phone. "We have to go."

"Wait," Wesley said. "There's more."

"More?" I said.

He nodded at the iPhone. "More."

[CHAPTER THIRTY-THREE]
OH YES,
THERE'S MORE

From somewhere offscreen I heard Squid saying something to me. I couldn't really make out what it was.

"Squid told you to take off your shirt," Wesley said.

When I looked at the screen, things had, uh, changed.

I LOVE YOU, CALLIE MIDWOOD...

GAZE UPON THE FACE OF LOVE!

I hit STOP, or I thought I did, but the touchscreen must not have been working, because the video kept playing. My face burned and my ears felt so hot that I thought they were going to explode.

"I didn't ... I mean ... I wasn't ..." I started to try to climb out of the car and realized that we were driving sixty miles an hour down the freeway.

"What are you doing?" Callie said, reaching back between the two front seats to grab me. "Are you crazy?"

My arm felt warm where she touched me. Then I realized something had changed in her face. Her cheeks were red and her eyes were shining like she might start crying. I'd never seen her like that before.

"Just keep watching," she said.

"What am I doing now?"

"Uh, Squid told you to climb up on a chair," Wesley said.

THERE'S SOMETHING
ELSE MY DAD TOLD ME . . .

COCK-A-DOODLE-DOO!

"Let me guess," I said. "Squid told me to crow like a rooster?"

"Actually," Wesley said, "he told you to bark like a dog. Apparently you think dogs say cock-a-doodle-doo. We'll work on that later."

I tried to shrink back farther into my seat. I was thinking maybe I could throw the iPhone out the window and nobody would know. "Are we done with this yet?"

Callie shook her head. "No," she said. "Listen."

And Nabeel's camera came back in for a close-up, as I heard my own hypnotized voice come out of the speaker again.

Callie and Wesley were both staring at the iPhone in my hand.

**THE MAN WHO'S BEHIND
ALL OF THIS IS . . .**

MR. MIDWOOD!

Wesley and Callie both got really quiet. Now I understood why Callie hadn't been anywhere when I woke up.

"We didn't believe you about Dad," Callie said. "But we went to find the Bug Man anyway, just to be sure."

"How did you find the Bug Man?" I asked.

"We Googled him," Callie said. "Got his address and drove over. And that's when we found out . . . it was true."

"He wasn't going for ice cream," Wesley said softly. "He was never going out for ice cream."

"I'm really sorry," I said. We drove along without talking for what felt like a long time. I wished that I could think of something to say, but I couldn't see Callie's face in the rearview mirror, and Wesley was just sitting there.

Finally Callie's eyes flicked up to the mirror. They looked glassy and blank. She started to slow down.

"Oh no," she said.

"What?"

Behind the car, blue police lights were starting to swirl.

CHAPTER THIRTY-FOUR

HAIL TO
THE CHIEF

Callie pulled over to the side of the road. I looked back expecting to see a police car, but what I saw instead was a big black SUV with a blue bubble flashing on top of it. There were two more just like it pulling up behind that one. A guy in a dark suit and sunglasses got out and walked over to Callie's car, staring in at me.

PETE SANCHEZ?

"Actually," I said, "my name's Pete Watson."
The guy touched the little microphone plugged

into his ear. He said something I couldn't hear. There was a long pause; then he looked back at me again.

PETE WATSON?

"Uh-huh," I said.

"Come with me." It wasn't a question. "There's someone who wants to see you."

I glanced at Wesley and Callie.

"We're his friends," Wesley said. "Where he goes, we go."

The man stared at him. "Stay in the car."

Wesley gulped. "Yes, sir."

I got out and followed the man in the black suit to the last SUV in the row of vehicles parked behind Callie's purple car. I figured if these were the same guys that Mr. Midwood had hired to kidnap Dad and put him into the CommandRoid to break the code, then it didn't matter if I tried to run from them or not. I wouldn't make it far on foot anyway.

The guy in the black suit opened the back door of the SUV and pointed for me to get inside.

There was another man waiting for me in there.

SON, DO YOU
KNOW WHO I AM?

[CHAPTER THIRTY-FIVE]

THE PRESIDENTIAL STRING THEORY

My first thought was that the president had very small hands.

Then I thought, *Can he tell that I'm thinking that?*

Then I thought, *Don't be stupid. The president can't read minds.*

But what if he could? What if—

I CAN'T READ MINDS, SON.

I stared at him. *How did he know that I was thinking that?*

And that was when the president leaned right in close to me.

PETE, YOUR FATHER WAS A GREAT AMERICAN.

WE NEED YOUR HELP.

"Wait a second," I said. "What do you mean, *was?* Is he . . . ?"

"He's trapped inside the CommandRoid with all our country's greatest secrets," the president said. "And we need you to get him out."

"Why me?" I asked, but I guess I already knew.

"You've got the code inside your head," the president said. He looked at his watch. "We've got one hour to rescue your father."

"What happens in an hour?"

"What?" The president scowled. "You don't know about the virus?"

"No, sir."

"Mr. Midwood doesn't want to crack the CIA's database. He wants to destroy it completely."

"How?"

"That's why Mr. Midwood hired the Bug Man," the president said. "To put a virus in the system. Why do you think he's called the Bug Man?"

"I thought maybe it was because he drove around with a giant bug on top of his car," I said.

The president just looked at me for a long moment. "Maybe we'd better find someone else."

I looked back at Callie's car up ahead and thought about her and Wesley, and my dad, trapped inside the system. They needed my help. I wasn't used to having anybody count on me for anything, but I realized that maybe this is how it feels when you're suddenly asked to do something that you've never done before.

"No," I said. "I can do it."

The president raised his eyebrows. "Are you sure?" He didn't look convinced. "Midwood and the Bug Man already have your father's CommandRoid. How are you going to access the data before the virus gets loose in the system?"

"Sir," I said, "all my life my parents have been telling me that video games aren't worthwhile"—I swallowed—"and that *I'm* not worthwhile. Well, today I have a chance to change all that."

The president frowned. "Your parents tell you that you're not worthwhile?"

"Well, not exactly," I said. "But they don't let me play video games as much as I want to."

"Ah." The president smiled. "I understand."

"You do?"

"Oh, yes." The president turned and gazed off into the distance. "When I was a boy, we didn't have much, but I had a piece of string. And boy, I tell you, I would play with that string all day if you let me. My parents would say, 'Put that string away! You'll never be president if you keep playing with a piece of string all day!' But do you know what?" He reached down into his pocket and held out his hand.

I looked at it. "Is that the same piece of string?"

"Of course not," he said. "What sort of idiot walks around with a fifty-year-old piece of string in his pocket?"

"I don't know, sir."

"Ah, well." He seemed to remember where he was, and slapped me on the leg. It kind of hurt. "You're a very brave boy, Sanchez."

"Watson, sir."

"Right." The president nodded thoughtfully off into the distance. "Do you own a watch, son?"

"Sir?"

"Every boy needs a watch. Take mine."

He took off the watch and gave it to me. I looked down at the bright red blinking display.

"It's in countdown mode," the president said. "I find it's useful in these types of situations."

"Thanks," I said.

"My pleasure," he said. "And Godspeed, Sanchez."

"Watson, sir."

But he was already turning away.

[CHAPTER THIRTY-SIX]
THE COCKROACH
IN THE
MIRROR

I got out of the car and walked back to where Wesley and Callie were waiting for me.

"Who was that?" Callie asked.

"The president."

"Of what?"

"The United States."

She stared at me long enough that I could count her eyelashes, twenty-six on each side. "What did he want?"

"He asked us to save it." That wasn't exactly true, but I needed something with some oomph to get us motivated. "Let's go."

"Where?"

"The City Convention Center." I checked the watch that the president had given me. "And we're running out of time."

Callie hit the gas, steering through traffic and tearing through yellow lights at all the intersections. That was when I saw the van with the giant cockroach on top coming into our rearview mirror.

"Look out!" I shouted. "It's him!"

The Bug Man came up so close behind us that I could see Mr. Midwood in the passenger seat.

"Hang on," Callie said. "This is going to get bumpy."

Okay. So car chases are cool in video games and movies, but I don't know how you're supposed to describe them in a book. In fact, just thinking about sitting there reading some description of two cars chasing each other around is putting me to sleep.

So instead we're going to do something that's much more fun than a car chase.

I call this mini chapter . . .

Lame Jokes
with Pete and Wesley

WHY DID THE KOALA FALL OUT OF THE TREE?

IT WAS DEAD.

WHY DID THE SECOND KOALA FALL OUT OF THE TREE?

IT WAS TAPED TO THE FIRST KOALA.

WHY DID THE THIRD KOALA FALL OUT OF THE TREE?

IT WANTED TO BE POPULAR.

That was when it all came back to me: the sticky note that had ruined everything! Just then—*screech!*

Callie hit the brakes and we all jerked forward in our seats.

"What are you doing?" I shouted. "We're nowhere near the convention center and we're running out of time!"

"I can't go any further." She pointed at the street in front of us. "Check it out."

I stared out the windshield, and my stomach dropped. At the intersection up ahead, a row of police cars with their lights flashing had formed a roadblock. The cops weren't letting anybody through.

"Throw it in reverse! Turn around!"

Callie shook her head. "I can't," she said, glancing in the rearview mirror. "Look."

I turned around. The Bug Man's van was pulled up right behind us with its front bumper touching the back of Callie's purple car, blocking us in. I could see Mr. Midwood and Stanley the Bug Man sitting there with big grins on their faces. There was no way out.

Meanwhile, two cops from the roadblock were heading our way, and they didn't look happy.

"Okay," I said, "let me do the talking."

[CHAPTER THIRTY-SEVEN]

ARMED AND DANGEROUS

The two cops who came over to the car looked like Muppets. Not the big-name familiar characters, but the ones you see singing in the background in the big musical numbers. One of them had a bald, melon-shaped head with a horseshoe of black hair wrapped around the sides, and the other had a long, skinny head with a tuft of red hair standing straight up.

"Is there a problem, Officer?" I asked.

Both cops ignored me, and the red-haired one turned his attention to Callie. "This street is closed off," he said. "We're looking for a group of terrorists disguised as . . ."

He stopped and stared at me, then glanced over at his partner, who was busy writing down the license plate number of Callie's car. Both cops whispered back and forth, and when the red-haired cop turned his attention back to me, he didn't look like a Muppet anymore. He looked like a cop who was going to toss me in jail and throw away the key until I was old enough to need an artificial hip.

"You," he said, pointing at me. "Step out of the car. And keep your hands where I can see them."

"What's the problem?" Callie asked. "Pete didn't do anything."

"Out of the car, *now*."

Climbing out, I tried not to freak. It wasn't easy. In fact, it was one of the hardest things I've ever had to do. It didn't help that Callie was gripping the steering wheel hard enough to make her knuckles go white, and Wesley looked like he was about to wet his pants. I tried not to think about the countdown on the watch, but I couldn't help looking at it anyway.

Less than forty-five minutes left. Whose idea was it to waste time on all those lame jokes?

The red-haired cop turned to his partner. "Is this the guy?"

"Looks like it." The other cop reached into his pocket and pulled out a folded sheet of paper. From where I stood I could read the words *ARMED AND DANGEROUS*.

Underneath it was a picture.

It was a picture of me.

[CHAPTER THIRTY-EIGHT]
SMILE, STUPID

It wasn't a very good picture. It was my school photo from last year. They'd taken it right after gym class, and I was still sweaty, and my shirt was unbuttoned one button too far. I had a dumb, crooked grin on my face like I'd been hit on the head by a fly ball. The photographer was the same guy who'd come to take our pictures every year, and the school must have gotten him at a discount, because he was pretty bad. To the girls he always said, "Hello, beautiful," and to the guys he always said, "Smile, stupid."

I wasn't smiling now.

"Pete Watson," the red-haired cop said, "turn

around and put your hands behind your head. You've got the right to remain silent."

"Wait a second," I said, "what did I do?"

"There's a warrant out for your arrest. Stealing government secrets. Making terroristic threats. And that's just for starters."

"That's crazy!" I felt one of them pulling on my hand, turning my wrist so they could see what was strapped to it.

"Fancy timepiece you've got there, Sonny Jim," the red-haired cop said. "Where'd you get it?"

"The president gave it to me," I said.

"The president of what? The committee for over-size wristwatches?"

"The United States."

The cops exchanged a glance. "Right," the melon-headed one snorted. "You're in enough trouble without the wisenheimer comments, don't you think?"

"Wait a second—it's in stopwatch mode," the red-haired cop said. "What's it counting down to?"

"Nothing."

"You're a terrible liar, kid, anybody ever tell you that?" They started pulling me toward their cruiser, and I heard somebody clear their throat behind me.

"Excuse me, officers. Perhaps I can be of assistance?"

Both of them stopped. Mr. Midwood was standing there, holding out a laminated ID badge with his name on it, stamped with a holographic image of an eagle. It looked pretty official.

"Agent Brian Midwood," he said, in an authoritative voice. "Homeland Security."

The cops looked at the badge, and then at me. "We were under the impression that this was a police matter."

"It's a federal matter now," Mr. Midwood said. "We'll take it from here." Then he glanced at me, and his voice was low, almost a growl. "Get back in the car. *Now.*"

I got in the back next to Wesley. Mr. Midwood got in the front seat next to his daughter. Callie stared at her father, but he didn't even look at her.

"Drive," he said.

[CHAPTER THIRTY-NINE]
ONE KILLION DOLLARS

Callie didn't drive. Not yet, anyway. Wesley stared at his father.

"Wow, do you really work for Homeland Security?" he said. "Do they let you carry a gun and stuff?"

"Don't be stupid," I said, which probably wasn't very nice because (a) Wesley *was* my best friend and (b) this was his father we were talking about, but I was pretty upset. "That badge is as fake as he is. In fact, I bet he's probably the one who sent in that picture of me to the police saying I was some kind of terrorist, so they'd catch up to us before we got to the convention center." I turned to Mr. Midwood. "Right?"

"You're a bright boy, Pete Watson," Mr. Midwood said. "Anybody ever tell you that?"

"Every now and then," I said, which was kind of a lie, but at this point I didn't see how it mattered. I nodded at Wesley and Callie. "Go ahead and tell them."

"Tell them what?"

"How you're planning to expose the identity of all of America's undercover agents and publicly humiliate the president and use that virus that you hired the Bug Man to put into the CIA's database to take over the world."

Callie stared at her dad. "Is that true?"

"I said *drive*." Mr. Midwood glared at his daughter. "It's a verb."

"Is it true?"

Finally Mr. Midwood shook his head. "No," he said. "It's not true. Not exactly."

"Then why *are* you doing this?"

"Why does anybody do anything?" Mr. Midwood shrugged. "For money."

"*Money?*"

"A lot of money."

"How much?"

"A lot, okay?"

"No," Callie said. "It's totally not okay. Because you're supposed to be our father. Which means that you're supposed to be good and decent—"

"And not mean and greedy," Wesley added. "And—"

"We're supposed to be able to trust you," Callie finished for him. "Which we obviously can't." She turned to glare at him. "So I want to know, Father. How much money does it take to make a supposedly decent and trustworthy man decide that he's going to put a virus in the CIA database and take over the world?"

Mr. Midwood rolled his eyes. "First of all," he said, "you're being melodramatic. I'm not taking over the world. Who would want to be in charge of the world, anyway? It's a headache—think of the maintenance fees." He sighed. "Second, if you knew my plan, you'd understand how ingenious the whole thing was." He turned to me. "I thought that you of all people would appreciate this, Pete."

"Why?"

"It's happening at GameCon."

"So?"

"They're unveiling a new game there at four o'clock." Reaching into his coat pocket, he pulled out a video game box labeled PROTOTYPE — TOP SECRET. "Meet Brawl-A-Thon SuperMax."

"Whoa," Wesley said, and caught himself. "I've never even heard of it."

"Nobody has," Mr. Midwood said. "The game designers are doing a surprise premiere today."

"What's so special about it?"

"It's going to be a multiplatform direct download," Mr. Midwood said. "Which means that anybody with an Internet connection can install it directly into their gaming console. And for today only"—his eyes gleamed—"they're offering it for free."

"Whoa!" Wesley said. "Let's go home and download it!"

"Hold on a second," I said, and turned to Mr. Midwood. "Why do you care about all this?"

"It's revolutionary," Mr. Midwood said. "Everybody who's anybody is going to be watching: TV reporters, technology experts, media people . . . I've heard the president himself might even show up." He grinned. "I couldn't ask for a better opportunity."

"For what?" Wesley asked.

And suddenly I got it.

"You're hijacking the game," I said.

"Bright boy." Mr. Midwood was still grinning. "You're absolutely right. The Bug Man put the virus in the CIA database, but that was just the beginning. I've used wormhole technology to link the database directly into the software architecture for Brawl-A-Thon SuperMax. Which means—"

"You'll be spreading the virus to every computer and gaming system in the country," Callie said.

"Not just the country," Mr. Midwood said. "The entire world. When they go after that free promotional download for SuperMax, they're going to be getting a lot more than they bargained for. I'll have infected every computer from here to Tokyo. Unless they pay me."

"How much?" Callie said. "You never told us."

Mr. Midwood took a long time before he answered. "One killion dollars," he said softly, savoring the words as they rolled off his tongue.

"There's no such thing as a killion," I said.

"That's where you're wrong," Mr. Midwood told me. "The killion is a number so large that it would literally kill you, which is why most people haven't heard of it. It was discovered by a man named Ian Frazier back in the eighties. Most mathematicians who have tried to count that high have started getting really sick and had to stop."

"Why would you want an amount of money so big that it would kill you?" I asked. "I mean, wouldn't that kind of defeat the purpose?"

"Not if you've got these." Mr. Midwood reached into his jacket pocket and pulled out the x-ray specs.

"So that's why you cared so much about those stupid things," I said.

"Wait." Wesley stared at them. "Those look different."

"That's because they're killion-proof," Mr. Midwood said. "They protect against extremely large numbers. So far they've only been tested up to a bajillion, but I'm sure they'll work just fine."

"You'll never get away with it," Callie said.

"We'll find out, in exactly"—he grabbed my wrist and looked at the stopwatch the president had given me—"thirty-seven minutes. So drive."

Callie didn't do anything for a second. Up ahead, the cops had pulled their cars to either side to let us through. Then she put the car into gear and drove jerkily between them.

Behind us, the Bug Man followed in his van.

He was grinning.

[CHAPTER FORTY]
MY BIG CHANCE

We got to the convention center ten minutes later.

"Remember," Mr. Midwood told me, "before you try anything, you're a wanted man. If you start running your mouth off to people, you'll just end up behind bars." Turning to his own kids, he added: "Kids, you don't want anything bad to happen to Pete, do you?"

"You're the worst dad ever!" Wesley shouted.

Mr. Midwood grunted. "Typical," he said, and waved us out of the car. Right behind us, the Bug Man swung up to the curb in his van and jumped out.

I looked at the crowds of people milling around outside. Earlier today, all I'd wanted was to come here and check out the new games. Now I wished I'd never heard of the place.

"Come on, hurry up," Mr. Midwood snapped. "I want you all to be there to see it when I bring the world to its knees. Stanley"—he turned to the Bug Man—"get the digitizer. Let's go."

We got in line. It took a long time. I kept looking at the stopwatch, the minutes ticking down. We weren't going to make it in time, and Mr. Midwood was getting irritated. He started pushing his way to the front until a fat security guard stopped him.

"Where's your admission pass?" he said.

Mr. Midwood flashed his ID badge. "Homeland Security," he said. "We're here on official business."

"All of you?" The security guard pointed at the Bug Man. "What about that guy in the jumpsuit?"

"He's an exterminator."

"And how about them?" He nodded at me and Wesley and Callie.

"They're my kids," Mr. Midwood said.

The security guard's eyes narrowed. "All of 'em?"

"Yes."

"Because the fat kid with braces and the girl

kind of look alike, but that other one"—he glanced at me—"doesn't look like you at all."

"He was adopted," Mr. Midwood said. He was starting to sound impatient. "Now if it's all the same to you—"

"Sorry." The security guard crossed his arms. "Nobody gets in without a pass."

Mr. Midwood turned to Stanley. "Can you fix this?" he muttered.

"Oh yeah." The Bug Man grinned and patted the pocket of his jumpsuit. "Trust me, I've got just the thing."

"Good, because we're running out of time. I'm going to get in position by the main entrance." He glanced at us. "Keep an eye on these little creeps, will you?"

"You got it," the Bug Man said, and Mr. Midwood ran toward the main entrance, leaving us there with Stanley.

That's when I saw my big chance.

"Stanley," I said. "You don't really want to do this, do you?"

The Bug Man turned to me, and his eyebrows went up in surprise. "What makes you say that?"

"How much is my dad paying you?" Callie chimed in, and I could tell she was picking up on my plan. "I mean, if he's getting a killion dollars for this, he's got to be giving you at least half, right? What is half of a killion, anyway?"

"That's none of your business," the Bug Man said.

"But it's a lot, right?" I asked. "I mean, it's a pretty big risk for somebody like you to take. He must be paying you really well."

"It's a *huge* risk, Stanley," Callie said. "If things don't work out, you could go to prison for a long time for this."

The Bug Man was just looking at us now. I decided it was time to make my move.

"You know," I said, "you could probably walk away from all of this right now and you wouldn't really be guilty of anything."

"Well," Wesley cut in, "except for—"

Callie kicked him. "Think about it, Stanley. What have you really done wrong so far?"

The Bug Man seemed to think about it. "I guess you're right," he said. "All I did was buy that CommandRoid 85 system. Which you sold to me, fair and square, for twenty dollars."

"Exactly," I said.

"So why don't you just let us go," Callie said, "and deactivate the virus?"

"You could be a hero," I said, "instead of the bad guy. Think of that."

"Write a different ending to the story, Stanley," Callie said. "An ending where one man can make a difference."

"There's only one problem with that," the Bug Man said, and I realized that he was smiling. "I've always hated heroes."

We stared at him. He reached into his pocket and pulled out a strange new controller that I'd never seen before. He whipped around and pointed it at the giant cockroach on top of his van and said something like . . .

NOW YOU'LL SEE HOW I LIKE TO PLAY!

CHAPTER FORTY-ONE

MASK CONFUSION

"Well," Callie said, "it was worth a shot."

We all stared at the van, where something *really* bad was happening. Here's what it'll look like in the game version:

BUGGED?
CALL THE
BUG MAN

"Um," I said. "Is that a giant mechanical cockroach crawling off the top of the van?"

"It's coming this way!" shouted Wesley. He looked at me. "Pete, do something!"

But the cockroach did something first—it charged at us. Callie, Wesley, and I jumped out of the way, and the Bug Man pushed another button on the controller. The cockroach went smashing through the outside of the convention center, leaving a giant smoking hole in the wall. Inside, we could hear people screaming and the sounds of expensive video games crashing and being broken.

But Callie didn't run. Mr. Midwood was back, and she walked right up to him.

"Dad?" Callie stared at him. "How could you do this? Even for a killion dollars."

"I told you, I needed the money," Mr. Midwood said. "How else am I supposed to pay for your college education?"

Callie froze. Then she did something that I didn't expect. She smiled. It was like through all the smoke and panic around her, a beam of sunlight shone down on her face.

"My real dad would have known that I have a scholarship to Harvard," she said. "A full ride. It's not going to cost you a penny."

Mr. Midwood frowned. "So?"

"So, that means you're not my real dad."

Mr. Midwood scowled.

OF COURSE I AM.
DON'T BE AN IDIOT.

"Oh really?" Callie reached out and grabbed her dad by the face and pulled. The mask came off in her hand to reveal . . .

MR. PRESIDENT?

"Wait a second," I said. "That's stupid! The president would never do something like this."

I reached out and grabbed the president by the face and pulled. The mask came off to reveal . . .

MR. YAPPERS?

"That's even stupider," I said. "No dog could have come up with such an elaborate plan."

"Border collies are pretty smart, though," Wesley said. "I once saw one doing calculus on TV. He had the chalk in his teeth and everything."

"Impossible," Callie said. "There must be one more mask here."

She grabbed Mr. Yappers by the face and pulled. The mask came off to reveal . . .

MRS. WERTLEY?

"But . . ." I couldn't believe it. "Why?"

"Oh, don't look so shocked," she said. "I already told you that my teacher's pension barely covers my retirement. And I had years of study hall to plan all of this. And"—she smiled—"a killion dollars is a killion dollars. After I found out that your father was a spy, I knew exactly what I had to do."

"What *we* had to do," the Bug Man corrected. "Right, partner?"

"Yeesh," Wesley said. "Really?"

"Oh no." I got a sudden sinking feeling in the pit of my stomach. "You have got to be kidding me."

[CHAPTER FORTY-TWO]
MRS. WERTLEY AND THE BUG MAN, SITTING IN A TREE?

"We planned the whole thing together," the Bug Man said. He was still moving the cockroach around inside the convention center with a big grin plastered across his face. "Which is why we're splitting the killion fifty-fifty as soon as this is over."

"Wait a second," I said. "What about this morning by my house, when I was stuck in the back of your van, and *you*"—I glanced at Mrs. Wertley—"came over and started hitting it with your copy of *Warriner's*? You acted like you didn't even know him. Unless . . ." I stopped. "You knew I was there. You must've seen me get in there."

"Bright boy, Pete," Mrs. Wertley said.

"You were sending him a message. Slamming

your book against the van. Telling him if he knew what was inside there, he'd be more careful about what he said. Telling him to . . ." I paused and stared at her. "Watch his words."

"Which he still hasn't learned to do," Mrs. Wertley said with a nasty, narrow grin. "Which is why I'm going to be keeping the full killion for myself." Her gaze darted over to the Bug Man. "Sorry, Stanley. Nothing personal."

For a second the Bug Man just glared at her, his lip curled back from his face in a nasty snarl. Then he smiled.

"I think you're forgetting something," he said, the grin spreading as he jerked the controller back in our direction again. "See, I always thought you might try to pull something like this. Which is why I've still got the giant mechanical cockroach."

From inside the convention center, the thing turned and started slamming its way back out toward us, knocking over what was left of the outside wall. Its shadow fell across us, and I could look up and see the layers of clockwork and machinery grinding away inside its undercarriage as it lunged closer.

"Wrong again, Stanley," Mrs. Wertley said calmly. "You see, I overrode that program too." Shaking her head, she reached into her pocket and pulled out a controller of her own. "And I've taken the liberty of unplugging your bug."

All at once the cockroach stopped moving. It stiffened for a second, then fell over with a deafening clang that rang out like . . . well, like a giant broken mechanical cockroach. Its legs twitched once and fell still.

The Bug Man stared at it. He opened his mouth and shut it again. His shoulders sagged, and he seemed to shrink a little inside his jumpsuit. Taking a couple of steps backwards, he kind of stumbled and then sat down on the curb, dropped the controller, and lowered his face into his hands. I wouldn't say that I actually felt sorry for him, but at least now I understood why he'd kept helping her, what he'd thought he was going to get out of it. Plus, it was a pretty cool cockroach.

Mrs. Wertley didn't even appear to notice. She was grinning up at the convention center and the hole that the Bug Man's cockroach had made in it.

"What about all this?" I asked her.

"This was just a bonus round," she said. "And you know about bonus rounds, don't you, Pete?"

I just stared at her. "How could you do this to my dad and I?"

"My dad and *me*," she corrected. "And it's a lot easier than you might think."

I checked the watch that the president had given me.

"Only seventeen minutes," I muttered under my breath. "We have to save my dad!"

"And the world," Callie said.

"Right," I said. "That too."

"How?" Wesley asked.

I turned back to Mrs. Wertley. There was only one thing left to do. It was a desperate plan, but right now I was a desperate man.

"Mrs. Wertley? I left my copy of *Warriner's English Grammar and Composition* in the van. May I go and get it, please?"

Mrs. Wertley's whole expression changed. The corner of her mouth started to twitch. Her left eyelid started going up and down. It was like there was a war going on inside her face, and nobody was winning.

"*Warriner's?*" she said. "Y-You left . . . your copy . . . of *Warriner's* . . . in the van?"

"That's right." I knew I'd said the one thing that she couldn't resist. "I'll just be a second."

"Dude," Wesley whispered, "what are you doing?"

"Trust me," I said, without breaking eye contact with Mrs. Wertley. "May I go and get it?"

"Yes." Mrs. Wertley nodded. "Go get it. But hurry back."

"Guys, follow me." We ran around to the back of the Bug Man's van, and I pulled out the only thing that I knew for sure could save us now. Two things, actually.

One of them I gave to Wesley:

The other I handed to Callie.

She just looked at it for a second, then said:
"What am I supposed to do with this?"
"Shoot me."

[CHAPTER FORTY-THREE]

A HERO
WILL
SHRINK

"Pete, no." For the first time, Callie looked scared—really scared. But not for herself. For me. "The virus is going to be loose inside the system. You'll be in terrible danger."

"Dude," Wesley said, "Callie's right! You'll be a grease spot!"

"That's why I need you to protect me from the outside," I said, nodding at the CommandRoid that I'd just given him. "Wesley, you're the best gamer that I know." This wasn't exactly true—I was actually way better at most of the games we'd played, except for Mr. Thumb Goes to Market—but Wesley needed a boost in confidence, so now was no time for total honesty. "Take this system and hook it up to the big screen where they're premiering Brawl-A-Thon SuperMax."

"I've never played this version before!"

"Nobody has," I said. "It's brand new. But if I'm going to stand a chance in there, you're going to have to help me get inside."

Wesley's eyes got really wide. "What if I can't move the controller? What if the game doesn't work right? What if you run out of extra lives?"

"Do your best." I tried to sound brave. "Don't kill me."

"Pete," Callie said, "please, there has to be another way—"

"No choice." Deep in my chest, my heart was doing its best to knock a hole right through my ribs. "We're out of time." I locked eyes with Callie. "Shoot me."

That was when she pointed the digitizer at me, closed her eyes, and pulled the trigger.

The first thing I discovered after Callie shot me with the gun was that being inside a video game is a lot less fun than being outside one.

Suddenly I was surrounded by big walls of words moving past me so fast that I couldn't even read them. I tried matching the code words, but I felt really . . . different.

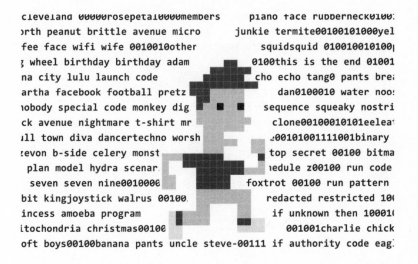

cleveland 00000rosepetal0000members
rth peanut brittle avenue micro
fee face wifi wife 0010010other
; wheel birthday birthday adam
na city lulu launch code
artha facebook football pretz
nobody special code monkey dig
ck avenue nightmare t-shirt mr
ll town diva dancertechno worsh
:evon b-side celery monst
plan model hydra scenar
seven seven nine0010000
bit kingjoystick walrus 00100
incess amoeba program
itochondria christmas00100

piano face rubberneck0100:
junkie termite00100101000yel
squidsquid 010010010100|
0100this is the end 01001
cho echo tang0 pants bre:
dan0100010 water noo:
sequence squeaky nostri
clone00100010101eelea
.00101001111001binary
top secret 00100 bitma
iedule z00100 run code
foxtrot 00100 run pattern
redacted restricted 10(
if unknown then 10001(
001001charlie chick

oft boys00100banana pants uncle steve-00111 if authority code eag:

I tried to look at my watch to see how much time I had left before the Bug Man's virus hit, but my arm wouldn't bend that way, probably because it was made of about three pixels. My only chance was getting help from the outside, but Wesley wasn't helping.

"Wesley!" I shouted. "Try hooking up a different joystick!"

But Wesley must have already figured that out, because from very far away I heard him shouting back that he was trying a better controller.

It didn't make much of a difference. I had no idea how much time I had left, and I didn't know where my dad was.

Meanwhile things were only getting worse.

```
cleveland 00000rosepetal0000members  _y piano face rubberneck0100:
)rth peanut brittle avenue microphone junkie termite00100101000yel
fee face wifi wife 0010010other guy mafia squidsquid 010010010100|
; wheel birthday birthday adam        01000100this is the end 01001
na city lulu launch code zebra 0 00100 echo echo tang0 pants brea
artha facebook football pretz        teely dan0100010 water noo;
1obody special code monkey digital ■  ■le sequence squeaky nostri
ck avenue nightmare t-shirt mrs.       santa clone00100010101eelea1
111 town diva dancertechno worship model home00101001111001binary
:evon b-side celery monster         ory 001001 top secret 00100 bitma
  plan model hydra scenario          1edule z00100 run code
  seven seven nine0010000 whiskey     foxtrot 00100 run pattern
bit kingjoystick walrus 00100101      cted redacted restricted 10(
incess amoeba program bolus          if unknown then 10001(
1tochondria christmas0010010 package       agent001001charlie chick
oft boys00100banana pants uncle steve-00111 if authority code eag:
```

The lines of code were closing in around me and tightening like a net. I knew it was only a matter of time before the Bug Man's virus got loose and erased every piece of data in the CommandRoid, and the fact that I couldn't even look at the president's stopwatch was making it even more frustrating.

I realized something.

This was all my fault.

I had blamed Mom for taking the twenty bucks from my jar, and I had blamed the Bug Man and Wesley and anybody else I could think of, but the fact is that if I hadn't been so determined to buy that stupid video game, then none of this would have happened.

The realization didn't make me feel any better.

cleveland 00000rosepetal0000membersonly piano face rubberneck0100:
>rth peanut brittle avenue microphone junkie termite00100101000yel
fee face wifi wife 00100100 guy mafia squidsquid 010010010100|
; wheel birthday birthday 000100this is the end 01001
na city lulu launch code zebra 010 00 echo echo tang0 pants bre;
artha facebook football pretzel legic steely dan0100010 water noo:
1obody special code monkey digital keyhole sequence squeaky nostri
ck avenue nightmare t-shirt mrs. cash santa clone00100010101eelea
111 town diva dancertechno worship model home00101001111001binary
revon b-side celery monster 001 top secret 00100 bitma
plan model hydra scenario 001 op schedule z00100 run code
seven seven nine0010000 whiskey tango foxtrot 00100 run pattern
bit kingjoystick walrus 001001010 redacted redacted restricted 10(
incess amoeba program bolus gradient 001 01 if unknown then 10001(
itochondria christmas0010010 package salt agent001001charlie chick
oft boys00100banana pants uncle steve-00111 if authority code eag

It was useless. I couldn't stay on top of it.

Why had I ever thought I could do this?

Then, in the middle of the codes and digits, I heard a familiar voice.

[CHAPTER FORTY-FOUR]
MY EIGHT-BIT DAD RETURNS

I don't really know how to describe how it felt running into Dad face-to-face in the CommandRoid universe. At that point I didn't really care how it happened; I was just glad that he was here.

"Pete, listen to me," he said. "It's going to be all right."

"How can you say that?" I asked. "I thought you weren't good at video games."

"I'm better in the eight-bit universe," he said, and waved me forward. "Come on."

From somewhere outside the game I could hear Wesley screaming that the controller was broken, that he'd never be able to get me out of there, but it was too late to worry about that now. Dad and I had our work cut out for us.

I had never seen Dad function in a video game reality before, but he was pretty good at it. I mean, when it came to moving stacks of text around and linking up all the codes so that they were reconnected, he was great. On this level it was a lot more like the CommandRoid universe, all eight-bit, but considering that the fate of the world's computer systems and information technology depended on it, it was pretty exciting.

All of a sudden I heard a sharp beeping noise.

It was coming from the stopwatch on my wrist.

We were out of time.

[CHAPTER FORTY-FIVE]
THE GREATEST CHAPTER IN THE WHOLE BOOK

That's when I realized what was happening.

The Bug Man's virus was breaking loose.

I can't describe what happened next. Fortunately I don't have to. I saved the best for last. In the digital version of this book, if you just hit the big red button under the screen, you'll be able to see it all for your-self in full-color high definition with stereo surround sound.

If the screen doesn't light up the first time, just hold the button down for ten seconds. If it still doesn't light up, start back at the beginning of the chapter and try again. It might be a little buggy.

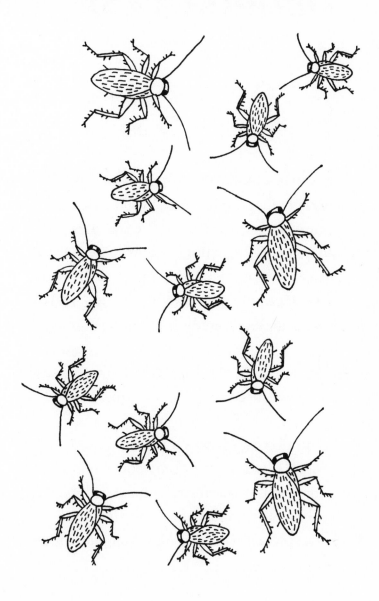

[CHAPTER FORTY-SIX]

WEAPON TEST

Uh, okay.

So until they get that fixed, this is what happened:

It was the most epic boss battle of all time.

If you play video games at all, you know that the most exciting part of every level is the boss battle, where you go head-to-head against whatever the big bad creature is on that particular level. In Brawl-A-thon, the Mega-MechReatures are the ultimate bosses, but at least you only have to fight one at a time.

Well, at this point the Bug Man's virus released *every single boss* in Brawl-A-Thon SuperMax, all at once.

Except in this case it was a little different.

"Uh, Dad?" I looked over at my dad, who was still standing there with his arms full of text, trying to put the code words together. "What is that exactly?"

We both stopped what we were doing and stared

at the other side of the screen. It was a big screen, but we could see very clearly what was happening.

"It's them," Dad said. For the first time, he looked really worried. "They programmed themselves into the virus."

He was right. Standing there inside the game with us were Mrs. Wertley, the Bug Man, and Mr. Yappers. Except that they'd been transformed by this level of the Brawl-A-Thon universe into eight-bit versions of themselves.

Mrs. Wertley had a giant mechanical praying mantis body with scorpion pincers and an electric stinging tail. The Bug Man had sprouted dozens of wiggling legs and was already scurrying across columns of code words in my direction. Mr. Yappers had become some kind of dog-shark MechReature with laser eyes and a long, extendable tongue. I figured the Bug Man had probably done the programming back before Mrs. Wertley double-crossed him, because he seemed more than happy to be helping her out here in the virtual world.

"Dad, what are we going to do?"

"If we shut it down now, we might still be able to stop the virus before it spreads through the entire game to all the computers and game systems in the world."

"How?"

"Pete." My dad looked at me. "Did I ever tell you that your name is an anagram?"

"For what?" I asked. "Teep?"

"Pete Watson," Dad said. "Weapon test."

"Okay." I nodded. "That's cool. But—"

Dad glanced down at the blocks of text scattered everywhere. "Words are our weapons," he said. "Let's put them to the test."

I didn't need any more encouragement than that.

Together we started picking up all the code we could find and throwing it at the virus versions of Mrs. Wertley, the Bug Man, and Mr. Yappers. It wasn't as hard as I thought it would be. I must have been getting used to moving as an eight-bit character.

At first, nothing happened.

Then everything got worse.

[CHAPTER FORTY-SEVEN]
BOSS BATTLE

It started when I clobbered Mrs. Wertley with a big slab of computer code. Instead of dying or exploding, her praying mantis body burst open and a dozen more versions of her came pouring out in every direction, replicating themselves around us on all sides. I realized with a shock that each one was carrying a copy of *Warriner's English Grammar and Composition*.

"How did you do that?" I asked.

"We're a virus, you idiot!" the Wertleys all said in one buzzing voice. It was like being lectured by a swarm of bees. Really smart bees, or at least ones that thought they were smarter than me. "The more you fight us, the more we're going to keep spreading through the software of the game!"

She was right. Dad was trying to go after Stanley the Bug Man, and the same thing happened to him. The Bug Man just became a dozen versions of himself, and they all started lining up blocks of text around us, trapping us inside. The way they were building the walls reminded me of wasps—or termites.

"That's why it's called SuperMax," the eight-bit Wertleys buzzed. "We're building a high-security prison around you. Once you're trapped inside, you'll never be able to disrupt the virus's spread."

"We can make you suffer," the Bug Men droned.

I wanted to tell them that if they wanted to know about real suffering, they ought to take a look at the Bug Man's heartbroken self, sitting on the curb outside the convention center next to an out-of-commission giant mechanical cockroach. "So you failed," I said.

The Wertleys all turned to look at me angrily. "What makes you say that?" they droned.

"You said you were doing it for the money. I guess they never paid you the killion dollars after all, huh?"

It was probably the wrong thing to say, but it got a reaction. Suddenly the Wertleys and the Bug Men stopped building walls around us, and they all came angling straight at me like a swarm of hornets. Somewhere far away I heard Dad tangling with a giant cloud of Mr. Yapperses.

We were out of options. Bending my elbow in a way that I hadn't been able to just a few seconds earlier, I glanced down at the president's watch, and for the first time I realized that there was a little switch on the side.

I pushed it, and the face of the watch flipped open. Inside was a tattered old piece of string along with a note that said:

Sanchez. This is the very first piece of string I ever owned. Use it to tie yourself to a better future. I'm "knot" kidding! Sincerely yours, the president.

Without thinking, I threw it at the swarm of Wertleys.

"You have to be kidding me," the swarm said. "A piece of string?"

"I didn't think it would work either," I said, "but I had to try."

But there must have been something about that string, because the second that it hit the swarm, it came to life, wrapping itself around them and tying them up in knots. The harder they fought, the more tangled up they got.

The next thing I knew, Dad and I were flying straight upward, blasting off the last screen and rocketing headlong into a brand-new environment like nothing I'd seen before in video games or the real world.

"What's going on?" Dad shouted.

I looked around slowly, taking it all in.

"I think we just leveled up," I said.

[CHAPTER FORTY-EIGHT]
SDRAHKCAB

This is how you know you're in trouble: you look around and realize that you're the only eight-bit characters left in existence.

Dad and I were standing in the middle of what looked like a huge factory. Everywhere we turned, giant machines with sprockets and conveyor belts were belching out versions of Mrs. Wertley, the Bug Man, and Mr. Yappers. Except they weren't the chunky, old-school graphics we'd been dealing with on the last level. These versions were slick, 3-D, digitally rendered characters complete with shadows and muscles and facial expressions, and they looked totally ready to kick our butts.

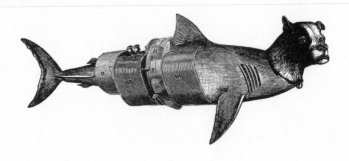

"Got any more of that magic string?" Dad asked.

I shook my head. "Got any more inspiring ana-grams?"

"Nope."

"Then I guess this is it."

"I guess so," Dad said. "Hey, Pete?"

"Yeah?"

"I just want to say, you're really good at this." He gave me a brave smile. "Whatever happens, you fought hard."

"Thanks, but this whole thing is my fault. If I hadn't sold your CommandRoid to the Bug Man—"

"That doesn't matter now." Dad held up his hand and rested it on my shoulder. "I'm proud of you."

Maybe it was hearing him say that, or the fact that he put his hand on my shoulder, but all of a sudden I had an idea. My mind went back to Wesley's basement, when I'd been trying to play Brawl-A-Thon 3000 XL.

"Hey, Dad," I said. "Remember *Superman: The Movie*?"

He blinked at me. "What's that got to do with . . . ?"

"Hang on," I said. "From here, things are going to get really weird."

Which was kind of the understatement of the year, I know, but when the swarms of Wertleys and Yappers and Bug Men attacked us, I knew what I had to do.

"Sdrawkcab klat," I said.

Dad's brow scrunched up in confusion. "What?"

"Sdrawkcab," I said. "Sdrawkcab klat."

Then he understood. I'd been hoping that with his mind for anagrams, it wouldn't take long to figure out what I was really telling him.

"Ho," he said, and smiled. "Sdrawkcab. Ti teg I."

"Gnikrow s'ti kniht uoy od?" I asked.

"Ti ekil skool." He nodded. "Flesruoy rof ees!"

In front of us the swarms of attackers had already started reacting to what we were doing, jerking away from us as if we'd suddenly gone radioactive.

"What is this?" the Wertleys screamed. "What are you saying? Those aren't proper words!" Their voices rose to a whole new level of sheer panic. "They aren't in *Warriner's English Grammar and Composition!*"

Dad pointed. "Ti thgif ot woh wonk t'nseod ehs!"

"Gniog peek," I said to my dad. "Kool!"

Talking backwards was having exactly the effect that I'd hoped it would. Everywhere we looked, time was turning itself in the opposite direction—like a movie running in reverse. The swarms were being pulled back into the machines that had spawned them, like bugs being sucked into a vacuum. The Yapperses and Bug Men got tangled together in a huge cloud as they disappeared.

The last thing I saw was the swarm of Wertleys

fighting to hold on to the grammar books they'd brought with them, and then they were gone too.

Dad let out a sigh of relief. "Krow dlouw taht wonk uoy did woh?"

"Emag oediv a morf ti denrael I." I grinned.

Around us the screen was changing again, and I saw the word rising up, ten times bigger than ourselves:

!SNOITALUTARGNOC

It reversed itself in space, but I already knew what it said:

CONGRATULATIONS!

Everywhere I looked, the architecture of the game was being restored around us, walls of words reorganizing themselves into neat rows. Dad stood there with his arm around my shoulder, and we watched the database being reassembled, solidifying into a new landscape of perfectly organized code.

And then—blackness.

[CHAPTER FORTY-NINE]
I SAID I WAS SORRY, OKAY?

When I opened my eyes, Dad and I were sitting in the middle of the City Convention Center, surrounded by people, cops, security guards, and reporters. Everybody was shouting questions at us, and I had no idea how to answer any of them. For a second I just wanted to put up my hands and shout, "Gnihtyreve nialpxe nac I! Kcab dnats tsuj, ydobyreve!"

But that would've been weird.

Then, through the crowd, I saw a figure coming toward us.

PETE, ARE YOU OKAY?

Except, you know what? Callie doesn't really look like that. It's time I got rid of that picture anyway. It's embarrassing. I guess if I had to show you what she looks like, the artwork would probably be more realistic:

It still doesn't really look like her. I'll have to keep practicing.

"I'm all right," I said.

"So . . ." Callie glanced up at the big display screen, which had gone solid blue, like the monitor does when you shut the system down to reboot it. "Did you beat the game?"

I glanced at my dad and smiled. "Something like that," I said.

"I'm glad."

"Me too."

There was a long, funny moment where we just kind of looked at each other, and then Wesley ran over, pushing his way through the crowd. He still had the old CommandRoid controller in his hand.

"Dude!" he shouted. "That was so awesome! We saw the whole thing down here!"

"Really?" I glanced up at the screen. "Yeah, I guess you would have." Then, turning to face the crowds of people around us, I asked, "Where are Mrs. Wertley and the Bug Man?"

"The Secret Service has Stanley in custody. As far as Mrs. Wertley goes, they haven't caught her yet, but it's only a matter of time."

"Wow," I said. "So much for a killion dollars, I guess."

"Pete Watson?" a voice said from behind me. "We'd like a word with you."

I turned around and felt my throat go dry all of a sudden. Two men in dark suits were standing there, staring right at me. In between them was a middle-aged Asian guy in jeans and a T-shirt.

"I'm Shigeru Miyamoto," he said. He pointed up at the big screen. "That was my new game you just destroyed."

"I'm sorry," I said. "But—"

"Now hold on," my dad said. "Pete's been through a lot today. I'm his father. If there's any trouble, I'm the one you want to deal with."

"Then you'll probably be interested in knowing," Mr. Miyamoto said, reaching into his pocket, "that I'm prepared to offer your son a lucrative deal as a beta tester for the rebooted version of Brawl-A-Thon SuperMax. It looks like we still have some bugs in the system." He smiled and held out an envelope. "I think you'll find the offer to your liking."

"Oh." My dad took the contract and opened it up. "Well, that's . . ." He kept reading. There was a number at the bottom of the page that made his eyebrows go up about three inches. He swallowed hard, and when he tried to talk, his voice sounded funny. "This is a lot of money, Mr. Miyamoto."

"Video games are serious business, Mr. Watson."

"You don't have to tell me that," my dad said. "Well, Pete, what do you say?"

"What else *is* there to say?" I said, and held out my hand to shake with Mr. Miyamoto. "Game on."

[CHAPTER FIFTY]
THE SKINNY

We stepped outside into the late afternoon sunshine: Wesley, Callie, and me. The Bug Man might have hated heroes, but I have to say that from where we were standing, being one felt pretty good.

Speaking of the Bug Man, you can probably guess the rest of the story, but if not, here's what my dad would call "the skinny."

THE BUG MAN was arrested on charges of building a giant remote-control mechanical insect and turning it loose in a public place. And also for distributing false information about termites.

And for creating a virus that almost—but not quite—brought the computers of the world to their knees.

He was taken to jail,

I'M INNOCENT, I SWEAR!

where he continues to serve a life sentence, probably with a dartboard of Mrs. Wertley's face taped to the wall in his cell.

The real MR. MIDWOOD, having no idea that his identity had been stolen by Mrs. Wertley, was still playing softball while all of this happened. He only found about it later on the evening news. Because in real life he was just a businessman and not a spy, it was all a big surprise to him—especially when he found out that my dad really did work for the CIA.

MY DAD went back to work for the government, and what happened after that is kind of a secret. I don't even know that much about it, but what I do

HMMM.

know is classified. I will tell you that it has to do with anagrams, and a new eight-bit computer program that he's creating based on Mr. Thumb Goes to Market. Except this one has a few unexpected levels.

MRS. WERTLEY actually escaped in the confusion. Her whereabouts, along with the location of Mr. Yappers, are currently unknown. But the last anybody heard, she was traveling with a rogue syndicate of retired teachers who have turned to high-tech computer crime to fund their international travel.

As for WESLEY, CALLIE, and ME? Well, let's just say things worked out well for all of us. After I went to work for Shigeru Miyamoto testing the beta version of Brawl-A-Thon SuperMax, I told him that I knew a couple of people who were as smart as I was, and almost as good at gaming. Mr. Miyamoto hired all three of us to go back in and work on the new eight-bit "retro" version, for a rebooted version of the CommandRoid due out next Christmas. So keep your eyes open for it.

Wesley's doing the sound effects. I'm doing the graphics. And Callie's designing the new digitizer for it. Turns out she's pretty good with that stuff. Who knew?

Best of all, we get to be characters in it:

In the deluxe digital version of this book, the program will probably already be included, so you'll be able to pick whoever you want to be . . . although I'm pretty sure everybody will want to be me, so you'll just have to take turns.

Oh, and it turns out that the shade of lipstick Callie was wearing that day is called "red."

I guess sometimes things are simpler than you think.

THANK YOU.
ANY QUESTIONS?

BONUS!

TURN THE PAGE FOR A SNEAK PREVIEW OF THE GAME!

"It's the game of the year—even though it hasn't come out yet!" —*Gamer's Monthly*

ULTIMATE BRAWL-A-THON: YAPPERS' REVENGE

THE BRAWL-A-THON LEGACY GOES TO A WHOLE NEW LEVEL OF EIGHT-BIT AWESOME!

• DEFEAT **MECHA-YAPPERS** as he attacks the secret government labs in the desert with laser eyes and unstoppable tank treads!

• Join your friends in fighting the Robo-Roaches of Doom!

• Defend your city as you launch rubber-band Wesley missiles at the floating head of Old Lady Blah-Blah and her Hypno-Eyes of Death!

Remember, ULTIMATE BRAWL-A-THON: YAPPERS' REVENGE is the only game that comes with hand-carved retro-style joysticks and the exclusive "Pete Sanchez" presidential stop-watch—guaranteeing nonstop ticking-clock action as you struggle to defeat forces you can barely control! Hand grenades! Hand cramps!

MAKE NO MISTAKE: THIS IS THE GAME YOU'VE BEEN WAITING FOR!

So this holiday season, burn your old Christmas list! Wad it up and set fire to it! You're not going to need any of that junk anymore! This year, the only thing that matters is ULTIMATE BRAWL-A-THON: YAPPERS' REVENGE! It's the greatest video game of all time!

Well, I guess you get the idea. That's pretty much the whole book. I'm not sure if I really got to fifty thousand words, or fifty pictures, but once my publisher gets the technology to put in all the graphics and music and everything, I don't think anybody's going to miss the extra words. I figure most of my readers will be too busy playing the game and wondering what kind of awesome ideas I'll come up with next.

Meanwhile I'll probably be on the cover of a lot of magazines and doing all kinds of TV interviews, so you should probably hold on to this version of it for when it becomes a collector's item.

But that's just my opinion.